# CELEBRITY

# SuperHERO

# A KPOP ROMANCE BOOK

Celebrity Superhero

Jennie Bennett

*To my imaginative children, never lose your sense of wonder.*

Celebrity Superhero

A K-pop Romance Book

Text © 2017 Jennie Bennett

Cover Design © 2017 Jennie Bennett

Cover Photo © Depositphotos videodoctor

Font © Vernon Adams, Nicky Laatz, and Quick Stick
Productions

ISBN-10: 1548635901

ISBN-13: 978-1548635909

Editing by Precy Larkins

Printed in the United States of America

# Contents

# DAMSEL IN DISTRESS

"Anna, I can see why Sungwook is your favorite," Erin says, pausing the music video. "He definitely has the best chocolate abs."

My teeth sink into my bottom lip as I stare, almost squeezing the life out of Rosie, my Pomeranian-teacup poodle mixed dog. Whoever had the bright idea to chain Sungwook up in a bathtub, wearing an unbuttoned white shirt and jeans was a genius, but I'm dying to watch the rest of the MV. I adjust my glasses and tuck my strand of purple hair behind my ear, eager to keep going.

The MV released today, and I want to soak it all in once before I watch it again. And again. And again. I'll probably learn the dance too, since that's what I do with all their songs.

I gently whack Erin's bony brown arm and lunge for the mouse. "Stop! Let's watch."

There is so much beauty I feel like my eyes might pop out of my skull. It's not just the five members of SUPER, although each one is amazing, but it's also the incredible videography and artistic storyline. Okay, and it's also the members of SUPER.

I'll never get why there are so many girls in my area who don't see these boys as attractive. Someone once told me I can see it since I'm Asian myself. I refrained from punching them in the nose, barely.

Thank goodness I have Erin to back me up, since she's black, they listen to her more.

I've spent the last three years of my short teenage life totally devoted to SUPER. From the moment their first song *Earth Shatter* dropped, I was hooked. Not only was the music, singing, and dancing completely on point but their superhero concept was mind blowing. Five tortured boys out to save the world from certain destruction one breathtaking song at a time? Swoon!

"Oh my gosh, Anna," Erin screams. "Did he just break the bathtub?"

I whack her again. "Shut up, I'm watching!"

Dark Doom, SUPER's evil nemesis, has them all trapped in various places around the world, and their girlfriend—yes, *their*, because they all appear to be dating the same person—is being dropped into a vat of boiling green liquid, and they must break free and save her.

Sungwook, who's naturally the best of the five, bursts his bathtub confines with his super strength and uses his super speed to navigate through a maze of mirrors, his chains still attached to his wrists.

Unique, who is sporting the most amazing bright blue hair in this MV, uses his laser vision to cut his ties and start his marathon across an endless desert.

Parkjae and E are entwined together in thick iron, but with their freezing and heating powers they shatter and melt their bonds, even though they're still lost in a cave.

Reign is trapped at the peak of a mountain, but Dark Doom doesn't know Reign's recently gained the ability to tunnel straight through to the ground.

All five boys, whose initials spell SUPER, gather and watch helplessly outside a blue force-field as their lover is dropped to her doom. Scenes splice through each of their faces as they sing, the camera panning out to the boys dancing in a reflective puddle.

Honestly, even if these boys weren't portrayed as having superpowers I'd still view them as completely otherworldly. There's no way that amount of talent came from Earth. Maybe there's a K-pop planet kinda like Krypton, and these boys come here and get their powers from our yellow sun.

I sit on the edge of my vintage refurbished white chair as the scene switches back to the girl. The hair-bow Parkjae gave her at the beginning of the MV falls from her silky hair and

Celebrity Superhero

disintegrates into black ash the moment it meets the death liquid.

Erin has grabbed my hand at some point, and I've been squeezing it so tight my knuckles ache. Even Rosie sits forward to watch more.

An army of ninja-dancing soldiers descend upon the K-pop group, and they must dance-fight to capture Dark Doom and shut down the machine, but that's when the video stops.

It's not over, just paused.

I start to hyperventilate as the infuriating circle of dots rolls around on my video. My eyes flit to the lower right-hand side of my screen and notice the wifi is showing zero bars. I bump Erin's hip, letting Rosie down to the floor. Erin lets me sit in the wheelie chair in front of my desk.

"This isn't happening," Erin says. "We have to find out if they save the girl."

"I know, I'm trying," I answer through gritted teeth.

I click on the wifi settings, my neck tense. Code red, major emergency, there is no wifi signal for our house at all.

"I have to go check the router," I say, standing so abruptly the wheelie chair crashes into my bookshelves.

"You mean this?" My mom has entered the room, and she's holding the router hostage in her hand.

"What are you doing?" I cry, my nerves so amped up I feel like I might burst. "There's thirty seconds left of this music video and—"

"And," Mom breaks in, talking louder than me. "Our guests are going to be here in half an hour. You promised you would clean the toilets before then."

"Mom, seriously, thirty seconds!" I hate that I sound like a whining kid, but this is life or death.

"Great," Mom says. "Then you'll have time to finish watching it after you're done with the toilets." She looks at my friend. "Sorry, Erin, I'm afraid you'll need to go home."

Erin glances at me and motions with her finger like she's going to text me later. She'd better.

I watch helplessly as she leaves the room, heartsick that the new music video will have to wait. Usually, I single-handedly give them thousands of views in the first twenty-four hours simply by having two videos on a playlist that loops. As long as I'm not logged into an account, YouTube counts each one as a watch. Yes, I've researched it. Yes, I'm obsessed.

The bathroom connects my room and the guest room. There's a sink and mirror for each side, with the toilet and shower in the room behind it. Apparently, it's called a Jack-and-Jill bathroom, because my mom says so. Opening the cabinet under my sink, I pull out the toilet brush and cleaner.

Mom is an interior designer, so everything in our house is either a tone of white or gray with

16

reclaimed wood accents and clapboard. Even the blue paint in the living room has a gray base tone to it. It's pretty, but it's also muted.

Sometimes I think about painting my room neon purple just to get some color into my life. In fact, that's probably why I dyed the single strand of purple in my hair, because then I could take my favorite color with me everywhere I go. Mom hates it, which makes it that much better.

She's the type who likes everything neat and orderly. Even the bowl of fancy soaps on the bathroom counter are positioned as if to look thrown in there, but I'm sure Mom spent half an hour making them look that way. Even though this is technically my bathroom, I'm not allowed to touch them. Instead, there's a liquid soap dispenser for me to use. I try not to roll my eyes every time I think about it.

I finish all the toilets upstairs in less than ten minutes like I knew I would. I try the wifi again, but Mom hasn't hooked it back up. She's in the kitchen making sure all her food looks like it came from a magazine spread, and cleaning the counters until they sparkle.

I could ask her to turn it back on, but I can tell she's gone full beast mode with the cleaning since people are coming over, and it's better to wait it out than to awaken the monster.

The brightest spot in my room is the bookshelf that houses rows of colorful manga. When I'm not watching SUPER, I spend my spare time reading about other Asians with supernatural gifts. Mom thinks I'm crazy, but I told her it's healthier to be invested in my fantasy world than drugs, and that shut her down pretty quickly.

I grab my favorite and most worn story off the shelf, Rosie standing at my heels. I love that Rosie follows me everywhere. Mom was the one who adopted her from the shelter, but as soon as she came home we connected and now she's my dog. She gets snippy when anyone else tries to hog me for too long.

A soft knock at the door makes me turn, my dad standing in the frame.

"You might want to take your book downstairs," he says, pointing to the volume in my hand. "Mom expects us all to be waiting for them to show up."

Dad understands how crazy Mom can get, and I'm happy to have the solidarity. I take his advice and follow him down the stairs to the living room where at least there's a cozy reading corner chair, even though I can't mess up the throw blanket that accents the white fabric. I tend to sneak messy snacks into that corner, anyway. What's a good book without food?

I tuck my feet under my body, and Rosie assumes her usual position next me, her floofy white hair tickling my arm. I try to allow myself to get lost in the tales of people with supernatural powers, so I can forget about the friends visiting from our motherland, Korea, to stay for a whole week. I haven't seen them since they left the good ol' U.S. of A. when I was six.

Celebrity Superhero

Beyond the fact that real life people are going to kill my time with fictional characters, I know I'm going to be pushed together with their son that's my age—a kid I only remember as a bully.

The last time I saw him, he stole my extra-precious Disney Princess locket. Did I mention I was six? That necklace meant the world to me.

Also, my parents are determined I marry this guy. Which, ew.

Seriously, from what I remember, he was super ugly. He had weird hair, and he smelled funny.

"Anna, put the book away, and send Rosie in the backyard. They're going to be here any second," Mom says from the kitchen.

Riiigght, like they were going to be here twenty minutes ago? I know I've been reading for way longer than the appointed time they were supposed to be here. I pretend to not hear her. Again.

"Anna," Mom calls, this time coming into the living room and waving a frantic hand. "I see their car in the driveway. Get the vase!"

I roll my eyes and slide out of the chair, but I don't put the book on the shelf. I do kick Rosie out, but I still intend to come back to my chair and keep reading before they've finished their awkward hellos.

These are not my friends but people my parents used to hang out with. Did I mention it was a decade ago?

Mom's already informed me that I will be polite no matter how boring it gets, and I have informed her that's impossible.

She can yell at me all she wants, but I plan on retreating to my room directly after dinner. I'm only sticking around that long because I've been told that my prized manga collection will be taken from me if I don't.

I pick up the white porcelain vase and hold it gingerly in my hands. What Asian buys a ceramic vase for other Asians? It's totally stupid.

Celebrity Superhero

Like, they couldn't pick up this exact thing in Korea?

No. They have to come to Portland, Oregon to get something Mom found in a, quote-unquote, thrift store where the items cost three times their actual value. But I saw the *made in China* sticker. It would be faster for them to go to China, honestly.

Maybe I'm being harsh, but I already know how much this week is going to drag.

"You're here!" Mom says in Korean, opening the door then pulling her friend into a hug.

Dad is there as well, giving his pal a bro-hug followed by a fist bump and some other weird handshake I can't bear to watch. It's gross when old people try to act young.

I try not to sigh too loud as I look anywhere but at the front door.

"Come in, come in," Mom says.

My foot taps on the hardwood as I wait. Can I hand over this vase now and get back to my book?

22

"Anna, you remember Mrs. Choi?"

"It's a pleasure to meet you," I rattle off in Korean, studying the ceiling.

Good thing I was raised speaking Korean, or else this would be ten times worse than it already is.

"And you remember Caleb, right Anna?"

Since I'm obligated, I lower my gaze and fix my eyes on the Choi's only child. My jaw drops as the vase slips from my hands. I've lost all muscle control. Time turns to slow motion, leaving me frozen in place as my thoughts start spinning.

Caleb is not who I remember.

Instead of the little brat that made me cry, I see a demigod. Hours of YouTube videos flash before my eyes, K-pop ringing in my ears.

Caleb is *not* Caleb. Caleb is Sungwook from SUPER. How did my parents not know that Caleb is the boy that hangs on the corkboard in my bedroom? For crying out loud, it was the only K-pop picture Mom allowed me to put up!

Celebrity Superhero

I mean, I guess I knew that Caleb was this guy's English name and not what he was given at birth, but no one could warn me? If I had known, I would've put on something nice and done my hair. I'm out of contacts, but maybe I could find some old ones or figure out how to go blind. Instead, I wonder if I still have Dorito dust on the corner of my mouth.

He's going to hate me without knowing me, run away, and forever remember me as the dork he met once at a family gathering.

Except…

My parents want me to marry him, don't they? Done. I take back every bad thing I ever said about my parents. They chose my future husband just right.

I unfreeze as some sort of scream/gasp/strangled-cry escapes my throat. One end of the vase is about to touch the floor, ready to shatter across the entryway. Next thing I know, I'm falling backwards. Waving my arms through the air as if I can right my balance.

24

I'm not sure what happened since I was standing just fine, but time goes from slow-motion to normal speed the second I land on my rear. My hand is scraped from catching my fall, but other than that, I'm unhurt.

It takes me a full minute to understand what took place, but I'm pretty sure it went something like this:

1. See Caleb—uber hot Asian pop star whom I've loved ever since SUPER debuted.

2. Have a freak-out panic attack and drop an expensive vase.

3. Get pushed away by said Caleb. Uber hot Asian pop star touched me, and I missed it.

4. Watch as Caleb catches expensive vase and saves my life.

It makes zero sense. In less than ten seconds, Caleb assessed the situation, pushed me out of the way, and kept the vase from breaking. It's not possible when one considers human reflexes. That was a superman-like, lighting fast reaction. Kind of like his character in the music videos.

Celebrity Superhero

Caleb stands over me with the vase tucked under his arm. One of his eyebrows is raised, and for a second, I think he's going to reach out his hand to help me up. But he doesn't. Instead, he says, "You always were clumsy."

I blink, trying to process his words. After seeing him for the first time in a decade, he's called me clumsy. What the crap is that supposed to mean? I was six the last time he saw me. SIX!!!

Granted, he was the same age so it's not like he made the wisest judgments either. This is the chance to start over and we have a whole week together. Oh my goodness, I have a whole week with my favorite celebrity in the entire universe. This is going to be amazing! I guess I can forgive him for one rude comment, considering we're going to be husband and wife.

I stand with no help from anyone in the room since they're all busy congratulating Caleb on his amazing catch. I'm tempted to congratulate him, too.

"Anna," Mom says, her voice all sugar. "Would you give Caleb a tour while we chat with his parents?"

Um, yes please! Time alone with Caleb? She doesn't even know how incredible a proposition that is. I'm just wondering how my parents never realized that my childhood friend is a huge star. I guess they're too preoccupied with whatever it is they spend their time on. I don't really know because I'm busy doing what I want.

*Okay, Anna, play it cool.* Keep the feelings down. This is a guy you like, but don't know. And he might hate you before you've had a chance. No need to get all worked up.

"Yeah, sure." I look at Caleb. "Do you wanna see your room?"

He crosses his arms, brooding. I guess that's a no.

Mrs. Choi nudges him. "Go on."

He lets out an exasperated sigh and stumbles after me. We walk to the kitchen and I point up the stairs. "You're up here so—"

27

Celebrity Superhero

"Let's get one thing straight," Caleb says, cutting me off.

I stop. His tone is not good. "Okaaay...?"

"We're not hanging out this week."

Ouch. Stake right to the heart.

He points back at the living room. "I'm only here because this is the time I have to spend with my family. Whatever you think you're doing, un-think it."

And a successful slaying of all my pride.

Turns out I was wrong about Caleb. All this time I've been watching him from afar, dreaming of meeting him. I imagined this beautiful, mind-blowing experience where we spot each other from across the room and fall in love.

From all the countless hours I've spent on YouTube watching him in interviews and interacting with the rest of SUPER, I thought I understood him. But seeing him in person is a totally different experience. I should have known it was all an act for the cameras. He really is the same kid who bullied me and stole my necklace,

28

and it took me less than half an hour to figure that out. How could I be so disillusioned?

This is why reality sucks. I hate it because it never lives up to my imagination. If Caleb thinks he can push me around, he's got another thing coming. No one, not even my favorite idol, treats me that way.

"What?" I say, spitting the word. I cock my hip and rest my hand on it. "I wasn't thinking anything. Other than the fact that you're a guest in my house and I'm trying to be a good host. Forget that. You can find your own way around."

I march back into the living room and snatch my book off the side table where I left it, and then run upstairs, slamming my door behind me.

Ugh. This was not how things were supposed to happen. I was going to be the one telling Caleb that I wouldn't be his chaperone. He wasn't supposed to be Sungwook, and I wasn't supposed to already be in love with him.

## Celebrity Superhero

It's stupid because he doesn't know he's been my obsession. He just waltzes in here and assumes he's better than me. I won't take it.

His paper face is staring at me from the poster on my cork board. I take it down and hold my hands at the top, beginning to rip through his perfectly coifed hair. My nails crumple the glossy surface, but I can't make myself do it.

As much as I want to totally loathe and reject him for being a jerk, I know that the idol I adore is in there somewhere. As long as I don't think of Caleb as Sungwook, I can pretend they're two different people. It's Caleb I have a beef with, and I'm not going to let him pierce my thick skin.

Jennie Bennett

# FITTING INTO THE CAPE

My heart pounds as I lean against a brick wall and gasp for air. I've been running for so long my thighs feel like jelly, but I can't quit yet. That thing, whatever it was, is still after me. If I can just make it to the sanctuary around the next corner I'll be safe.

I beg my legs to move, to leap across the space and find shelter, but the alleyway stretches longer and longer and my lungs are burning so hard they're about to light on fire.

Then Sungwook is there, right between me and the corner that will save me. I reach for him, but he's too far away. He stands with his legs apart and arms folded, a dry ice-like vapor flowing off his body, glowing lime green in the moonlight.

"Help me!" I yell to him.

His eyes narrow, a smirk on his lips. I glance back, knowing that whatever chased me will soon find me, thanks to all the noise.

"Help you?" he says in his harshest tone. "I'm the thing that's out to get you."

I gulp and back away, hands up in defense. It's too late. All the running and hiding was in vain.

Sungwook spreads his arms and flashes open his palms, shooting ice from his hands. A thick, frozen cube incases me so I'm no longer able to move. The sound of Sungwook's laugh echoes around us, sounding a lot like someone knocking at my door.

"Anna," Sungwook says, his voice an octave higher and feminine. "It's time to come down."

I startle, bolting upright in my bed. It was all a dream, but my body doesn't know that yet. My heart is still pounding, sweat beading on my brow.

I search for my glasses but they aren't on my bedside table. I squint at the clock. Crap, it's already noon. I didn't mean to sleep in that long. It just happened.

The rapping on my door gets louder. "Anna. Lunch. Now!"

Seriously? "Just a second, Mom, I'll be right down."

I run towards the bathroom, my need to pee trumping all other thought. When I wrench the door open, messy hair and all, there's a figure standing on the other side. I might be blind, but I can tell my family members from a stranger, and this blurry person is in the shape of Caleb. I'm so used to this bathroom being my own that I hadn't considered the fact that he's in the connecting guest room.

"What are you doing in here?" he asks.

Oh gosh, can he turn off his ego for, like, five seconds? I spent so much of the previous day trying to avoid him that he must not have known we share a bathroom. At least he spoke to me in English. I guess he did live here for a time so he's bilingual like me.

"I need to pee. I thought that's what bathrooms are for," I blurt.

It hurts me that I have to pull out my snark, because part of me is still drooling over him. As much as I thought I could make my feelings for his online persona go away, they haven't. That's not going to keep me from being myself, though.

"Gross," he mumbles.

I want to make it to the potty room, but I don't really want to do it with Caleb still in here. I also feel defenseless without my glasses.

"Um," I say, trying not to do the bladder dance but still shifting my feet from side to side. "Have you seen my glasses?"

"Isn't that them?" Caleb says, pointing at the ground. Or at least I'm pretty sure he's pointing at the ground.

I have no idea why they'd be there unless he knocked them off the counter.

"I. Cant. See." Boy's dense.

He scoffs. "They're right in front of you. Take two steps forward."

Yeah, real helpful, because he can't just pick them up and hand them to me.

I stride forward and *snap*. Nooooo! I just stepped on my glasses. They were really cute too.

"I can't see!" I yell again.

Caleb is laughing. I don't need my vision to know that.

He reaches down and picks up my glasses. From the outline, I can tell they're not going to be wearable. I steal them from his grasp anyway. When I put them on, one of the lenses is missing. I can only see out my left eye. The right side is hanging all screwy. It's making my head hurt. I have to close my right eye so I feel like I can see.

Great, of all the times to run out of contacts. There's an old pair of glasses in my dresser, but they're straight from my middle school years and no one makes good fashion choices at that age.

Caleb's still laughing. "I'll see you at lunch," he says, waving to me as he leaves.

Grr! Who cares about him? I'm not trying to impress him anyway.

After relieving myself, I go back to my room and pull out my old glasses. I still don't know what I was thinking when I got them. They're perfect large circles and green camo. Yep, worst decision ever. They don't make my vision as sharp, but they'll suffice until I can take a shower. I really hope my contact order gets here soon.

Celebrity Superhero

I catch a glimpse of myself in the mirror on the back of my door.

Wow. It's a good thing I've decided I'm not going to impress Caleb. My black hair is all tangled on the side where I slept. Now with my weirdo glasses I look like a genuine sideshow. Caleb's already seen me so I go with it. Maybe it'll help the pain in my heart over losing my idol crush.

I strut into the kitchen. That's right, strut. No use in hiding it.

I look right at Caleb as I sit, running my fingers through my knotted hair with a flourish. I don't lose his eye contact as I adjust my gargantuan glasses so they fit just right.

"What on Earth, Anna?" Dad says. "We were all waiting for you."

Caleb hasn't stopped watching me so I make sure to look at him as I speak. "Thanks to a certain someone, I stepped on my glasses."

He flinches, narrowing his eyes. "It was my fault," he admits. "I should've been more careful. I'm sorry," he says in formal Korean.

Who is this person and what did he do with Caleb? I glace at his parents who are beaming at him with pride. Okay, I get it. He's playing the role of filial son and all that jazz.

My eyes flick away. One thing I can say for sure is that he cares about his family. They're the reason he's here, and he's good to them. My cheeks heat up as I think about how embarrassing I've been in front of people he cares about. I hate that he's gotten to me with a single sentence, again.

I move the food around my plate, stabbing my metal chopsticks into my rice bowl a little harder than necessary. I've zeroed in on a single grain sitting on the edge of my bowl, and I keep poking it, hoping it'll eventually stick to the end of my chopstick.

"Anna, watch out!" Caleb says.

I hit my chopstick against the bowl one more time, and the edge of the dish cracks and clatters to the table. My spine goes rigid as I raise my eyes.

"I tried to warn you," Caleb says.

I blink, my throat going dry. He totally saw my bowl was going to crack before I did. "How did you know?"

Caleb shrugs. "I heard it splitting."

Heard it? From across the table? I was sitting right here and I didn't hear a dang thing.

"Anna," Mom says, "watch what you're doing."

I can't believe I just broke Mom's nice china. She's about to get really upset, I can tell. But that's not my first concern. I have to get out of here so I can think.

"Excuse me," I say, getting up from my chair. "I don't feel well."

Caleb heard my bowl breaking. Heard it! My breathing speeds up. It can't be true, but I don't know what else to think. He caught the vase way faster than any human, and now he's hearing sounds better than my dog. Could he...?

I shake my head. Not possible. People like that don't exist in the real world.

Dad wrinkles his eyebrows. "You haven't touched your food."

Mom lays her chopsticks to the side of her plate. "Why would she eat if she's not feeling well? Look at her!"

I push my glasses up my nose, remembering what a hot mess I am.

"Go get some sleep," Mom says, waving an exasperated hand.

I try not to, but I can't help but watch Caleb as I leave. He looks worried. Perhaps he's worried I'll discover his secret?

This requires research. I bow to my family and the visitors before running upstairs.

Thank goodness Mom set the wifi back up. I open my laptop and start by watching the newly released MV, searching for any sign that what I'm seeing is real and not made up. It could be. Really. Some of the special effects are obvious, but not all of them. That puts me in the same position I was two seconds ago.

So the internet wasn't any help, what else is new? I still can't shake the feeling he's otherworldly somehow.

I spend most of the day watching K-pop vids with my headphones in, thinking about Caleb.

Celebrity Superhero

Erin texted me once, but I told her I would be busy until our guests leave. I have no idea how to tell her about Sungwook, or the fact that he's a jerk. I've gone downstairs twice, once for leftover food, and once for a soda. Luckily, I wasn't caught since they all went out to sight-see.

Now that my stomach is full, and it's night, the sleepiness is winning. I sludge to the bathroom to brush my teeth and wash my face.

As soon as I get inside I hear talking coming from Caleb's room. Light seeps through the door to the tile. He's probably still messed up because of the time change from Korea.

I shouldn't, really. I'm not a stalker. But Caleb is right here and he's talking so loud he's practically begging me to listen in to his conversation. I hope he's distracted enough that he doesn't notice me tip-toeing closer.

My ear presses to the chilled door. Good thing it's hollow, I can hear right through.

He's speaking Mandarin, dang! I forgot his K-pop group does Chinese promotions, too. I guess he's tri-lingual, thanks to his training. I really wanted to know what he was saying.

40

I'm about to walk away when I hear him switch to English. "I have to fix the jewelry. It's important."

Jewelry? What kind of jewelry?

"I asked you to have the stuff ready for me. Don't play dumb. I'm speaking English so there's no misunderstanding. Now tell me."

Wait, what if Caleb really does have superpowers? If he does, this could be someone like Dark Doom who's stolen something from him. That would be so exciting.

"I know what I said," he continues, "I changed my mind. I tried not to let the past get to me, but it already has. As much as I've resisted, I'm weak."

The past? Weak? What could that possibly mean? I wonder if his supernatural powers aren't working as well here. Maybe the jewelry is some kind of amulet that restores him to health.

"Hang on a second," he says.

I go stiff. Shoot. Did he hear me? I hold my breath, trying to be as soundless as possible.

The door swings open from his side and I stumble into his chest. He catches me with an

41

arm around my back and my weight causes us to spin around like we're dancing. I cower into his rock-hard abs a second before meeting his eyes, embarrassed he caught me listening in.

He holds my gaze, and I take him in fully. His perfect dark hair is wet like he just got out of the shower, and his shampoo smells like dark chocolate. I can't help but focus on his Adam's apple, my gaze tracing the lines up to his masculine chin. I swallow but don't shift, worried one wrong move will disturb this moment.

"I'll call you back," he murmurs, letting the phone drop from his ear.

He studies my face with dark eyes that sparkle, even though it's night and I know he's going to say something rude. I don't want to hear it so I straighten my spine and push out of his embrace.

He speaks anyway. "You weren't supposed to hear that."

This time, I don't feel hurt. Rather, I feel validated knowing I was right. He's for sure hiding something.

I'm really not in the mood to pick a fight, so I concede. "Sorry about that."

He breathes out hard through his nose, his jaw tight. He's trying to hold his anger together, but why? He had no problem being a jerk to me before.

"Just," he says, "don't do it again."

I stumble as he pushes me back into the bathroom, shutting the door in my face. Ah, there's that guy again.

If anything, I'm resilient. I will figure out what his deal is, but that means I need to spend more time with him. There has to be something I can do to make him like me.

"I can help you," I say, opening the door.

Caleb's back is to me, his shoulders stiffened. He doesn't turn around. This is going to be a long shot, but I have to try.

I need to convince him that he needs me. "I've lived in Portland most of my life. I know it better than most people. If you need someone to show you around or take you somewhere…"

I know it's lame, but I'm doing my best.

He doesn't move, the silence ballooning between us. I guess that's my answer. It was worth a shot anyway.

"Why should I let you?" he says after a second, tipping his head so I can see the edge of his profile.

Yeah, I got nothing. I-just-want-to-be-with-you doesn't seem like the right thing to say at the moment.

"Because," I whine, scrambling to come up with something. "I'm so adorable."

He turns a bit of his shoulder so he can see me better.

I can't believe I'm going to do this, but I'm pretty desperate.

My fists go to my cheeks. A little *aegyo*—or acting cute—can go a long way. His mouth softens, just a touch.

"Bbuing, bbuing?" I venture.

That's all it takes—the corners of his mouth turn up, the sparkle in his eyes intensifying. I could look at that face all day.

He turns around and grips the door so tight his muscles flex.

"I'll let you go with me on one condition."

Bubbles are forming in my stomach, tickling my insides, but I try not to appear too eager. "What's that?"

He narrows his eyes, his mouth a straight line. "We go tomorrow night, after my parents are in bed."

I pretend to fake-punch him. "Don't want to be seen in public with me, eh?"

He swings the door so it only frames his face. "Exactly."

With a click of the lock, he's gone.

Ice king has returned! I knew he couldn't stay away for too long.

My eyes naturally close as I sigh. Why do I let myself like him? It just brings me pain.

I wasn't going to dress up. It's not like changing my appearance is going to make Caleb think of me any differently. But the whole time I'm in the shower I keep thinking about the moment he smiled, and how his whole face transformed. I really, really want to see that smile again. Maybe if I attempt to look hot it'll work.

Yeah, I'm already laughing at myself.

I take time picking out my outfit anyway. I find a purple short-sleeved blouse, with sheer fabric, that Mom bought me hoping I'd be more girly. She got the color right, even though it's not usually my style. I throw on some white shorts that make my legs look longer. She would be so proud.

Rosie is looking up at me with her head tilted like she's not sure what's happened to her favorite person. It's been a while since I put on anything other than a t-shirt and jeans.

Patting Rosie as I walk by, I go back to the bathroom and dig through a box where I used to keep my contacts and find some old unopened ones that work. They'll probably burn my eyes by the end of the day, but they'll suffice. I even curl my hair and put lip-gloss on. This deserves a selfie since I never dress up. One with a classic peace sign, and then one that's just me.

Mom calls me down for breakfast, and I don't want to keep anyone waiting today so I stuff my phone in my back pocket and exit my room. Walking down the stairs in my wedge sandals is harder than I remember. I take each step slow, holding onto the railing as I go.

The first time I look up from my feet, I see Caleb standing in the living room watching me. His chest is puffed out and his mouth is closed like he's holding his breath. I would say he's mad, but that's not quite the expression I'm sensing. More like...confused? My focus goes back to my feet. I can't handle him staring that way.

"Breakfast!" Mrs. Choi reminds me when I reach the bottom step where Caleb has stayed, waiting for me.

Why would he do that? I can't figure him out.

Caleb walks with me side by side to the kitchen. Weird. I steal peeks at him, but he never looks my way.

He sits across from me, still not making eye contact. I really shouldn't care about the things

47

he does, but I do. He doesn't even know how much I care.

"Today we were thinking of going downtown," Mrs. Choi says.

Great. An awkward day with virtual strangers and Caleb visiting places I've already been. Whoopie!

Mrs. Choi claps her hands together and looks at her son. "But, we want you kids to do something together."

Caleb stiffens, his fingers gripping the table. "No," he says to his mom, not taking a second to think it over. "I came here to be with you."

She pats his arm, smiling. "Caleb," she answers in a serious mom-tone. "We've been here three days and you've hardly said a word to Anna. You can see me in Korea. Here, you can be whoever you want to be. I want you to experience what it's like to be a teenager and hang out with other kids your age."

"You can even borrow my car," my dad says.

I start to choke on my rice, but when I reach for my water, I knock it over, sending liquid dripping off the side of the table and onto my shorts. Thankfully, the paper towel holder is right behind me on the counter.

There's no way this is happening. My father, however humble, is proud he owns a Dodge Challenger SRT-8 with all the bells and whistles. He bought it during his mid-life crisis, and he never—*ever*—lets me drive it. I don't blame him since it's a fifty-thousand-dollar vehicle. If it gets scratched, he'll have a heart attack.

This has to be because he's trying to impress the Chois. Either that or he's ready to pick out our wedding date.

"I hear Caleb is a very good driver," Dad adds.

Taking the dripping paper towels, I throw it in the trash a little harder than necessary, spraying Dad with a few drops. Dad thinks boys are inherently better at everything, and driving tops that list.

"Uh," Caleb says, looking between Dad and me. "I have my license, but you don't have to do that. If we need to go somewhere, we can take a bus."

"Nonsense," Mr. Choi bursts out, "You two should have more freedom than that."

Caleb squirms in his seat. I do my best to keep the bubbles in my belly from running over. I have to get a hold of myself and push down these feelings. He made it really clear he doesn't like me around him, at all. Why would two nights of sleep make a difference?

I take a seat at the table again. My shorts have a few wet spots, but they'll dry quickly.

"Here's the keys," Dad says, putting them in Caleb's palm with both hands. He takes a second to grip Caleb's hand tight. "Be nice to her, son."

I try not to laugh out loud as I read the pain on Dad's forehead. He's not letting go of Caleb's hand even though Caleb is trying to pull away. Glad to know that even though Caleb's a boy, Dad still doesn't totally trust him with his baby.

Caleb looks at me like I'm going to save him, but I'm still trying not to laugh aloud. He turns to my dad. "I will, I promise," he says.

Dad finally lets go, but the worry line is still on his brow.

Jennie Bennett

This day is going to be awesome. With all this time alone with Caleb, I can figure out what's really up with him and his superpowers.

Mom pushes us out the door before we've finished breakfast, Caleb's parents standing behind and nodding their approval. Even Rosie is sitting there watching us go, and she doesn't seem upset that I've leaving with someone that's not her, which is weird. Dad's the only one with a frown on his face, and that's because of the car.

All four of them stand on the porch waving to us as we drive away. They insisted we go and do something fun before they leave the house. It's really embarrassing, but sweet at the same time.

Caleb looks really uncomfortable, even though the red bucket seats hug us. He's keeping his elbows in as he drives and looking forward, not even glancing in my direction. It's quiet, too, and I'm terrified to turn the radio on.

He has to know I was pushed into this, same as he was. The least he could do is try to make conversation.

51

Celebrity Superhero

Honestly, ever since I dressed up this morning, I've been acting like someone I'm not. Just because I have on a little makeup and short-shorts doesn't make me a different person. Our parents wanted us to have fun, so I'm going to enjoy myself. It's not like I expect anything from Caleb. The crush I have is entirely on my side. There's no way I'm going to change his feelings in a few days.

I open and close the glove compartment a few times, fidgeting as I try to loosen up. We haven't decided where we're going yet, but Caleb hasn't asked me for directions anywhere, so I assume he knows what he's doing. He drives with his hands tight to the steering wheel, and a glance at the speedometer tells me he's going five under the speed limit. There's a line of cars behind us, waiting for him to speed up.

"You know that pedal to the right?" I say, pointing. "It makes the car go."

A flicker on his brow before his face goes smooth again. Cold as stone, that one. There has to be a way to melt him a little.

"This car has a thing called a V8 Hemi. That means it's built to go faster than the average car." I smile, but Caleb isn't looking at me.

I only know that a V8 is powerful because Dad reminds me every single time I'm in the car with him. I can almost hear him telling me about how alive he feels when driving. Gag me.

Caleb is still frozen, the speedometer not moving an inch. Which leaves him open to more teasing.

"The funny thing is," I say, laughing. "The car was created to move. When it doesn't move, other drivers get upset. I promise pressing the gas won't make it break."

Caleb's hands grip the wheel tighter, his knuckles turning white. I'm having way too much fun bugging him about this.

"Oh, hey look," I shout, "a snail passed us. That has to be a record."

Caleb bangs a fist on the wheel. "Will you shut up? I don't know how to do this."

Hold the phone. "What?"

"I've only driven a car like three times. My parents are the ones who applied for an international license for me."

I'm a more experienced driver than Caleb? No way.

"Pull over, right now. I thought your parents said you were a good driver!"

Caleb isn't stopping. "I'm not," he says. "My manager drives me everywhere."

Funny that he would mention a manager. I don't think he knows that I'm aware of his career. I pretend I didn't hear that part.

"My dad is going to kill you if he finds out you don't know how to drive. Pull over, right now."

Caleb is still going straight. In fact, he hasn't turned once since we got in the car, except when he left the driveway. My dad had it backed in so Caleb didn't need to reverse at all.

I'm too afraid to ask the question on my tongue, but it must be said. "Don't tell me you don't know how to pull over."

A small laugh escapes as I say the words, but Caleb's face is blank. "I'm afraid to turn the steering wheel too much."

Oh, this is bad. This street ends in a couple of blocks.

"Okay," I say, making a split-second decision. "I want you to let go of the gas and I'll turn the wheel."

Good thing we're still in my neighborhood and not on the freeway.

"Are you sure?" he says, his voice wobbling.

"Let go, now!"

This time I don't wait for him to react. I grab his hands and guide us toward the curb. "The brakes, hit the brakes!"

For once he listens. I throw the car in park the second we're stopped, and lean back in my chair. I start to rub my palms down my face as I sigh, but stop when I reach my nose. Holy crap, I had these hands on Caleb and they smell dark-chocolatey like him. It's amazing. Would it be weird if I kept my hands on my face for the rest of the day?

Celebrity Superhero

I peek at Caleb over my fingers and notice he's still ignoring me. Yep. I'm weird.

"Okay," I say, clapping my hands together. "I'm driving."

Caleb's still stuck to the steering wheel, unmoving. I wave in front of his face. No response. Now I'm starting to doubt my superhuman theory. Would a superhuman be this terrified of driving?

There's only one thing to do. I peel off Caleb's fingers from the steering wheel one by one until he's free.

I'm about to give him his space, but he grabs my hand before I can move away. It's not romantic. It feels urgent, pleading.

"Did you see that?" he says, pointing out the window to a forest beyond the neighborhood.

I squint. I don't have the best vision in the world but with my contacts I can see okay, and there's nothing.

"Caleb, I don't—"

"Look, look!" he says, pointing faster. A bald eagle bursts through the tree tops and starts to circle upward.

I gasp. Whoa. How did he see that?

Now I'm freaked out. He's got to be some kind of *something*—I just haven't figure out what that something is yet.

# Finding Kryptonite

This is why I came, wasn't it? To be *sure*. I'm sure now. Funny how he can't handle turning a steering wheel, but he can hear a bowl cracking, and spot a bird in the middle of a forest.

I want him to know I know, but there's no easy way to go about that. Maybe if I ask him how he did it?

"I hate birds," he says, releasing my hand.

My fingers feel cold now that he's no longer clinging to me. I'm still leaning in his direction though, and I don't think I can ask him if I move too far away.

"Caleb, how did you see that far?"

There. It's out. No going back now. I wonder if he saves people in his free time, like a real superhero.

"Birds of prey are especially frightening," he says.

Is he avoiding the question? That wasn't even close to the answer I was expecting.

He looks in my direction for the first time since we got in the car, and our faces are nose to nose. He swallows and scrambles away, opening the car door as he goes. The only thing that stops him from landing on his butt is his grip on the car door.

"Are you okay?" I ask, leaning over the seat farther, still close to him.

His feet are backpedaling, and there's loose gravel on the street. He slips, almost doing the splits as he hangs onto the car door.

"F—f—fine. I'm fine," he says. He trips a little as he stands up, but recovers.

He walks around the car to my door, rubbing the back of his neck and muttering to himself. This is the first time I've seen him be anything other than totally in control. Strange.

Just before he gets to my door, he stops and looks at his hands. I have no idea what's going through his head right now. Maybe that whole thing with him not being able to drive and slipping out of the car was just because his powers aren't working right and we need to fix that amulet-of-power sooner.

Celebrity Superhero

I open my door before he gets the chance to touch the handle, and he barely misses jumping out of the way.

"Sorry," I say, scrambling to the driver's side. I want to hurry to whoever he was talking to last night so I can help him get better.

He's strapping his seatbelt on as I slide into my side. I'm ready to put the car in gear and peel out, but then I realize I don't know where to go.

"Where does this person live?" I say, focused on the road in front of me, even though we're not moving.

"Uh—" Caleb answers, his voice distant.

I nudge his shoulder with the tip of my finger. "We're going to see the person you were talking to last night, remember?"

"Yes," he says, pulling out his phone. "but—"

I raise both my eyebrows. I would raise just one eyebrow, but I've never been able to do that.

"Um..." he continues, tapping at his screen. "My GPS doesn't seem to be working. Do you know where 88th avenue is?"

Why're we going there? "Yeah, I used to live on that street. Why?"

That's the place where I knew Caleb as a child. Of course, back then I didn't know he'd be a huge star.

Caleb presses his lips together then releases them. He should not be allowed to do that so close to me, especially when I know I'm the only one thinking about us in any context other than friendship. But dang, that's hot.

"That's where my friend lives," he answers.

What if he discovered his powers when I knew him, and this person we're going to see is an old shaman in our neighborhood who taught him how to control everything? I think I remember another Asian family on the same street who had their grandma living with them. We must be going there now to speak with the wise mentor who helped Caleb in his path to enlightenment. I can't wait.

My family moved us out of the main city to a suburb so it takes a good half hour get to the address Caleb gives me. If he was still driving, we'd be dead since we have to take the freeway. At least I'm good for something.

Celebrity Superhero

"Oh," I say, parking the car on the street and shutting the engine off. "I remember this house."

Mostly because it creeped me out. There were so many trees I couldn't see the house. Now that I'm closer though, it's actually a nice single-story, white-siding home. The front yard is just a little overgrown.

Caleb doesn't wait for me to get out of the car but charges for the front door before I can unbuckle. I try to catch up to him, but my wedge heels are making it difficult. He's already rung the doorbell by the time I get there, tapping his foot like it's taking forever.

I smile at him and rock slowly to the balls of my feet. He's so focused on the door that I can watch him unabashedly. He's so much more beautiful in person. Seeing his face is one thing, but being close enough to feel his warmth, to smell his scent, to study the details of those amazing eyes and lips...it can't compare. I already know when he leaves I'm going to go through withdrawals.

In all the madness of him coming here, and being a jerk, and the superhuman stuff, I haven't had a second to really fangirl over the fact that he's next to me in person, and I get to enjoy it. If Erin knew this was happening, she'd kill me. She will never believe it. I'm still not believing it myself.

Let's be honest here. I'm head over heels for this boy. Even in all the madness, I have a real serious crush on him and not just an online infatuation. I've seen glimpses of the person I know underneath, the real Caleb. He's trying to hide it from me, but something happened yesterday and today he's softened.

He's such a mystery I wish I could figure out, but for now, I'm just going to enjoy watching him. This Sungwook is a picture of him I don't have to share with the rest of the world. It's just me and him with the sun shining through the tree tops. I snap a mental photo and store it in my happy place.

I think back to my childhood impression of him, and I'm glad I was wrong, about his looks anyway. He's so ethereally perfect. In fact, I'm certain it's one of his superpowers.

Celebrity Superhero

My feet go flat as the door opens. I'm standing to the side of the doorframe so I can't see who's there, but they're speaking rapid Mandarin and I don't understand a word of it.

Caleb pinches the fabric of my shirt and tugs me toward him. "Anna," he announces.

What the heck, this dude isn't an old lady. In fact, he's probably my age, and he's kinda cute. Dark hair sweeping over his forehead and clear brown eyes that reflect the light. Could he be superhuman, too? Like maybe part of a Justice League sort of thing.

"Anna?" the guy in the doorway says. "Anna Eom?"

I'm not sure what language to speak so I just nod.

The guy steps out of the door, right between me and Caleb. He looks at my face, all the way down my body, and then back up.

"Dang, Anna," he says in English. "When did you get so gorgeous?"

Heat rushes to my cheeks. No one's ever told me that before. He glances over his shoulder and says something to Caleb in Mandarin.

"Hey!" Caleb says, flipping the stranger around and grabbing onto his jacket.

I'm forced to step off the porch as Caleb holds him roughly. Although I don't know the language, the conversation is definitely a fight. The guy doesn't seem bugged at all, and he's saying something that's got Caleb all bent out of shape. If Caleb has super-strength, too, this won't end well.

Stranger dude says something to Caleb that calms him down, and I step back onto the porch.

"Is everything okay?" I ask, tentative.

Caleb pulls me next to him. "It's fine."

The stranger reaches out a hand. "Hi, I'm Shaun."

Glad to have a name with the face. Did I mention the face was good looking? Very good looking. It bugs me that I'm noticing it so readily in front of Caleb.

Shaun extends his hand, and I blush as our palms touch. Dang. Why is attraction so confusing?

I let go of Shaun's hand before I embarrass myself further.

Caleb says something angry to Shaun in Mandarin, and Shaun shoots me a wink. He leans in over my shoulder, despite Caleb being so near. "Don't mind him," Shaun whispers in my ear, "he's touchy." Whoa. Chills.

I stifle a giggle, feeling girly and flirty for once. It's nice to be liked, and I know all too well Caleb doesn't have feelings for me.

"Do you have the stuff or not?" Caleb says to Shaun in English. His tone is serious, so this must be urgent.

"Let's have a look," Shaun says. He offers me his arm "My lady."

I'm not sure I can stop blushing, even my ears are hot. It's sweet, and so, so perplexing. When I look at Caleb, I feel guilty, so I don't take Shaun's arm.

That doesn't stop Shaun, though. He places his fingertips in the middle of my back and guides me into the house.

Shaun gestures for me to sit on the loveseat, and then takes the spot next to me. Right next to me. Our thighs are touching. No one has ever given me attention like this. I scoot over because

Caleb is watching, but it's not like Caleb wants to sit next to me. In fact, he sits on the other side of the room, as far away as possible. It just confirms how Caleb feels about me.

"You must be a saint if you're hanging around Caleb," Shaun says.

I chuckle. "It's not so bad."

I'm glad Shaun hasn't closed the gap between us, but I feel a weird desire to slide back over to him. I don't.

Caleb stands, wiping his palms on his pants. "I don't want to be here longer than I have to."

Shaun points to a cardboard box sitting on the coffee table. "The stuff you need is in there. I got it ready for you after you called last night."

They're totally in some sort of superhero coalition together. I can feel it.

Caleb's nostrils flare as he stares at the two of us. What is up with that look? All I'm doing is sitting. Then again, it's not like he's had a glowing impression of me to begin with. I wait for him to give me another digging comment, but he doesn't. Instead, he directs his poison at Shaun in Mandarin. It's killing me that I can't understand the words even though I can tell Caleb's not happy.

"You can go do it yourself, right now," Shaun says in English. I'm grateful he's including me in this conversation. "Everything's in there, and I know you're capable."

Caleb shoots Shaun another death glare and picks up the box. Maybe it's like Superman-Batman thing where they're frenemies.

I start to stand because I think I'm leaving with Caleb, but Shaun takes my wrist and pulls me back to the couch. "He needs a minute."

Right. Caleb doesn't know I've figured out his secret, and he's probably trying to hide the amulet that helps his power. That's fine with me, as long as nothing hurts him.

"So, Anna," Shaun says. "You don't remember me, do you?"

I shift in my seat. Somehow, unconsciously, our legs are touching again. Do I have a reason to remember Shaun? I guess we lived on the same street when I was young, but it's all a blur. I only seem to remember Caleb. But maybe there

Jennie Bennett

was another kid that played with us too, and
maybe this is him.

Should I be honest? I suppose he has a
reason to remember me since he even knew my
last name. I want to lie, but I can't make up
memories that don't exist.

My words come out cautious. "No. I don't."

Shaun nods his head. "Figures, you only
cared about Caleb anyway."

So he knew the two of us together. I wonder
how I've been missing Shaun all this time.

"I was just the dorky kid who followed the
two of you around," Shaun says, giving a pretend
sniff like he's about to fake-cry. "Who would
remember me?"

Aw! Shaun looks all heartbroken and sad. I
can't let him be that way.

"I'll remember you starting now," I offer,
nudging him with my shoulder.

His eyes snap to mine. "Really?" Beautiful,
clear eyes.

I smile wide. "Really, really."

Our legs are still touching, and suddenly, I'm
aware of the intense heat passing between us.

Without Caleb in the room, I'm tempted to move closer. Goodness Shaun is hot.

"We should hang out sometime." Shaun pulls out his phone. "What's your number?"

I'm holding my breath, feeling all kinds of things. I don't know how to order these emotions. In any other circumstance, I would say yes. Even now, I want to shout my number as fast as I can and have him text me for good measure so I know he has it.

Today, however, Caleb is in the next room. It's not like I have any shot with Caleb, ever. It makes zero sense considering the way Caleb has acted toward me at this point. I mean, I knew he was kind of arrogant, but on YouTube, he was also cute, and funny, and just...my ideal guy.

Not to mention I feel like I'm on the edge of a breakthrough. I want Caleb to confide his secret to me. If he does, we'll be connected. Even if it's not romantically. I just want to help him.

So, although Shaun is really cute, and I'm attracted, I can't give him my number until Caleb leaves. I have to know how things are going to play out first.

"That's really sweet—" I say, but Caleb drops the box on the coffee table, cutting me off.

Caleb's face is stern, arms folded as he watches Shaun and me. "Let's go," he says to me in a monotone voice.

I give Shaun a sideways look, only to find our lips nearly touching. Shaun seems to notice and he inches forward like he might actually kiss me. This would be a bad way to have my first kiss. Not in front of Caleb.

I back up and turn my head, but there's nowhere to run unless I fall off the loveseat. Caleb takes hold of my wrist again and pulls me up just as Shaun's lips brush my cheek.

Now I'm in Caleb's arms feeling a bit like a toy being fought over between friends. The room is really tight and hot, and I can't think clearly. I shove Caleb away and walk out the door without looking back. Thank goodness I have the car keys so I can hide inside and hyperventilate.

My head bangs the steering wheel. What just happened? I can't process it at all. Shaun was going to kiss me, without my consent. That's not okay. He might be cute, but I'm feeling violated, which is probably why I pushed Caleb away.

Oh Caleb, my mystery boy. He saved me from that. He didn't have to. Maybe it's his super-power reflexes kicking in. The way I reacted, however, was even worse.

Leave it to me to wreck my reality just when it starts to get interesting.

# Facing the Villain

When it comes to fight or flight, my first reaction is flight. I'm tempted to drive away then lock myself in my room for the rest of the week so I don't have to relive that moment again.

But I have to be stronger than that. For Caleb.

"What's taking so long?" I whisper to myself after a few minutes.

The front door opens a second later as if Caleb heard me. Oh right—super hearing. How could I forget?

He slams the door as he gets in the car and doesn't look my way. I really screwed things up. He probably wants to get away from me as fast as he can.

I start back the way we came, but the usual freeway exit is blocked off. Some guys are putting tar stuff on the road, so it's going to be a while. That means I have to go all the way around. It's a pretty drive, but much longer.

73

Celebrity Superhero

It's so quiet I want to turn on the radio for background noise. If it were my choice, I'd connect my phone to the stereo and rock out to K-pop, but I have a feeling this isn't the best time for Caleb to know I'm a fan. It might be the thing that makes him explode.

We're passing by Forest Park, a reserve of land worthy of its name. Of course, most of Oregon is forest, but the trees are a bit thicker here.

"Pull over," Caleb says.

No way. I'm too afraid of what he might do.

"Please," Caleb says. "Pull over."

I'm thinking about ignoring him again when I remember he has superpowers. Probably best not to test his limits.

I don't look at him, even after we've stopped. "What is it?"

"Do you mind if we get out of the car? There's something I want to ask you, and I'd prefer it if we go for a walk."

Now? I'm trying to get home so I can avoid him as quickly as possible. Plus, wedge sandals.

74

I risk looking into his big sparkly eyes. The second I do, I know it's a mistake. I can't say no to him. I want him to be happy more than I want to be with him.

He gives me half a smile, and even that is blinding. "Please?" he says again in Korean.

I know very well that *please* in Korean is more than just please, it's begging. If only he knew he'd already won me over. I can't find words right now, so I swallow and nod at the same time.

He gets out, but my body is having difficulty moving from the chair because I'm still in shock.

Caleb opens my door, unleashing his full smile. How does he expect my brain to function? I'm already frazzled, and he's making it worse by being sweet. Getting out of the car is all a fog, but somewhere in there, Caleb has taken my hand.

We've started a down a trail in silence before awareness hits: Caleb hasn't let go of my hand.

All the times we've touched have been so chaotic, I've never processed what the feeling is like.

Celebrity Superhero

The stillness of the world around me leaves no room for distraction. Now I have no choice but to feel his skin. The warmth and strength of his hand in mine.

The feeling starts in my palm, which is flat against Caleb's. At first, it's a gentle tingle, a whisper of a buzz. As I stare at our hands, the intensity grows, stinging my nerves until it's like a spark lights up. That's when the heat hits.

A sensation like flames, simultaneously hot and chilling, twist up my arm until my heart is alight.

The blood-pumping muscle kicks into gear, working double time and affecting the rest of my systems. My breathing speeds up as those bubbles dance around my stomach.

I'm frozen, eyes wide, as the flames overtake me.

Caleb lets go and jumps back as if he's just realized we're touching as well.

I shove my hands in my back pockets so I'm not tempted to touch him again. It's all so temporary, I'll just torture myself if I get greedy.

We keep walking, a gentle breeze blowing through my shoulder-length hair and lifting my purple streak.

Caleb clears his throat. "I wanted to apologize about what happened at Shaun's house."

I narrow my eyes at him. Did he really just say sorry? I'm not sure I can trust that.

"Shaun can be a little forward," he continues.

Understatement of the century.

Caleb pulls at the collar of his shirt. "I wanted you to stop here because I didn't know when else I'd get the courage to tell you. It's okay if you don't want to talk to me anymore."

Don't want to talk to him anymore? Where is he getting that impression? Oh yeah, I've been silent since we left Shaun's house.

"I'm not upset at you," I offer. "I'm upset that Shaun would try that when I just met him."

"You don't remember Shaun?" Caleb says, stopping in his tracks. His voice is so incredulous I might think he actually cares about my reaction.

"Noooo?" I say, unsure of why he's suddenly acting like this.

Caleb looks away, scratching the back of his head. I try to peek around so I can gauge his reaction but he effectively blocks me out. Just like he always does.

Caleb stares at the canopy of trees. "You mean to tell me you haven't been getting the emails?"

And the winner of the random question award goes to Caleb!

"Emails? What emails?"

Caleb catches my eye for a quick second, but then I see he's not really looking at me—he's looking at *something* beyond me. "Run," he says, and takes off.

What the heck? He didn't answer my question. There's no way I can run in these shoes, but I have to follow. His parents would kill me if I lost him. I slip off the sandals and start to sprint into the trees. Broken branches and little rocks stab at my feet as I veer off the path to follow Caleb.

It's already too late though, because Caleb is much faster than me, almost superhuman fast. I wonder if he thinks he's taking it easy on a mere mortal.

The sound of brush cracking in my wake makes me forget the pain and run faster.

Great, now he's so far ahead I can't see him.

"Caleb?" I yell, but I'm running low in the oxygen department so I'm not very loud. I stop where I am and try to fill my lungs. "Caleb!"

A hand covers my mouth, a strong arm pulling me into a body. My instinct is to scream, but that's not working. I try to wriggle free, but another arm goes around my waist. I thrash harder, kicking the shin of my attacker, the heel of my foot digging in.

I hear a little yelp as my attacker's grasp relaxes. I spin around and put out my karate-chop hands, my shoes held out like swords.

Oh heavens, that wasn't an attacker all, just Caleb. He's holding his leg like I might have hurt him, though I have no idea how.

"Are you okay?" I ask.

Celebrity Superhero

He puts a finger to his mouth and shushes me. He points deeper into the woods and motions for me to remain quiet.

I'm not sure what's going on, but if he's worried, I know I need to be worried.

He gestures for me to follow him, so I do, getting deeper and deeper into the forest. We're walking around in so many circles I'm worried we'll get lost, but at least I have my phone in my back pocket if we need to get help.

He stops, studying a large bush, and then moves aside a big leafy branch. He takes my hand again, this time pulling me inside. What the—?

"Sorry," he says, crouching beside me until we're both squatting.

Man, this space is miniscule. Our shoulders are rubbing. Not that I mind.

"I think we lost them for now," he says.

Lost who? Shoot. I bet Caleb has an arch nemesis out there somewhere, and he's in trouble.

"Everything all right?" I ask.

Caleb peers out of the bush, keeping a lookout. "I could've done without you kicking me, but yeah."

My legs are starting to hurt, but I don't really want to sit in the forest ickies. Although, my feet are already a mess. Caleb's not breaking a sweat. What else is new?

I know we're waiting out the enemy or whatever, but my thighs are falling asleep.

"How much longer do we have to squat here?" I complain.

Caleb looks at me for the first time since he's crawled in, and all the air between us vanishes.

"Are you uncomfortable?" he asks, gently pushing my shoulder until my butt lands in the dirt. "Sit."

Oh man, pins and needles all down my legs. Even if I wanted to leave, I'm not sure I can walk. I take my phone out of my back pocket and set it on my lap.

"So, we're staying for a bit."

"It's safer this way."

Well, I'm already dirty. I'm not sure my white shorts will survive this as it is. Sitting doesn't feel that great, so I decide to lie down. I have to put my knees up to fit, but it works. Sunlight streaks through the foliage above me, sparkling dots of dust hanging in the air.

It feels weird with Caleb crouching like that. It would be perfect if he would just settle.

Maybe it's selfish of me—cut that—I know it's selfish of me, but I can't help but wonder what it would be like to have Caleb lying next to me, looking at the sky. There's no way anyone could see us in this bush unless they spread the leaves. Worth a shot anyway.

"Hey Caleb, the ground is nice and comfy."

He looks at me, evil eyebrow raised. All right, I lied. The ground is not comfy. I'm pretty sure there's a tree root in my back.

"Come on," I coax. "Relax a little. We're pretty hidden."

Caleb purses his lips. "Well, okay."

Holy frack, it worked! I keep my arms under my head and Caleb's elbow touches mine as he assumes the same position. There's not enough room for him to not touch me, but it still sends fire-ice things all through my nervous system.

"I'm sorry," Caleb says after a minute of silence.

Apologizing again? No way. I'm not sure what he has to be sorry about, but I guess it's good he's not being an unfeeling jerk like he was before.

"It's okay," I return. Because it is. Even though we're hiding from someone or something, I feel perfectly happy being with Caleb like this.

"I know…" Caleb says with a sigh. "I know it's not easy to be around me. There's stuff going on I'm not sure you understand—"

"Stop."

I thought my heart rate was elevated before, but now it's knocking on my ribcage. I don't want him to say anymore. He shouldn't have to utter it aloud.

"Caleb," I say, not sure how to say this without sounding crazy. The direct route is probably best. "I already know your secret."

I'm terrified of his reaction. I don't dare turn my head to see his face.

"How long?" he whispers.

Oh boy, I don't want to answer that, but he has a right to know. "Since you first came. Well, since this morning but I've been suspecting all week."

He lets out a long breath. "Did someone tell you?"

It's cute how he thinks he's hiding it. I can see right through him. "No. I figured it out."

Out of the corner of my eye, I see his head roll so he's facing me. I'm going to have to look at him eventually, so I do. He's staring at me, searching my face for answers. "And what do you think?" he asks, his words breathless.

That's a loaded question. There's so much I want to say to him, but now isn't the time. Him knowing that I know is enough.

"I think it's awesome."

Caleb turns fully on his side. "I came here wanting to hide it from you, but I guess I'm not good at that."

I laugh. He didn't hide it, at all. "Who else knows?"

He shrugs. "I haven't actually told anyone, but if you figured it out, then I guess everyone knows."

No. I just happen to be more astute to supernatural experiences. Anyone else would call me insane. "I doubt it. Don't worry, I won't tell anyone if you don't want me to."

Caleb nods. "That's probably best for now. I'm glad you know, it makes things easier. I've been meaning to ask—"

He cuts off mid-sentence and puts a finger to his lips. I can hear murmuring just outside the bush.

"Leave no leaf unturned," the voices say. "He has to be here somewhere. Remember, don't hurt him."

Oh my gosh, what am I going to do? Caleb can defend himself, but I don't want him thinking he has to defend me as well.

Footsteps draw closer, the sound of bushes being whacked as they go. I really, really don't want to be in the middle of this when they find us.

Celebrity Superhero

Caleb holds onto me so I can't leave, but his eyes look terrified. There's a rustle, and a bird hops into our bush. Caleb shoots up, screaming.

He stands for a second, and then tries to hide again. I'm pretty sure we're busted. I have to help him. I can distract his nemesis long enough until he does something.

Good thing my legs have come back awake or else running would be difficult. I stand, leaving my shoes behind so I can go faster.

"Hey!" I yell at the people outside, who are all wearing black medical masks on their faces along with black hoodies and beanies. "I'm the one you want!"

Then I dash away.

My calf muscles are protesting, but I push past the pain. I want to say it's enough. That I can make myself strong like the characters I love to read about.

But I'm not.

Fingernails dig into my back, shredding skin. With one pull, I'm captured. I jerk away, but it's no use—all I do is ruffle the nemesis's hat.

"Anna!" Caleb yells.

My aggressor whips me around in time to see Caleb jump towards him. I'm hurled to the ground, hands scraping the pebbly path. Caleb takes off into the other direction, the masked guys following.

Terror freezes me to my spot. What if they're superhuman too?

I can't just leave Caleb. He could get lost—he doesn't know the area like I do.

"Aish!"

I forget my bruised body and charge after them, keeping my distance. I'm not sure I could keep up anyway.

Caleb fakes right and one of his assailants trips. Since I'm behind, I cut through the brush, gaining me an advantage. My feet are all torn up, but that's not what's important.

There are two more guys still hot on his tail. Caleb rolls and trips Dude Number Two. Dude Three doesn't waste time striking, but Caleb dodges.

"Anna, get the car running!" he yells.

But...I don't know what direction the car is in.

Dude Three has Caleb backed against a tree. "Anna, run straight forward! The car is out of the tree line."

Okay, maybe he doesn't need me, since I'm the one who's confused.

I'm about to leave when Dude Three lunges at Caleb again. Caleb dodges, and the guy hits the tree behind him. My hands go to my mouth, shock holding me still.

Dude One is back, black hairs falling out of his cap as he lumbers toward Caleb.

"Anna, now!"

Right, the car. But I'd have to run into the fight to get to it.

"Anna!"

*Get a hold of yourself,* I tell myself in Korean. *All you have to do is run straight through the mess like Caleb asked.* I run, watching someone hit Caleb's shoulder as I pass by. He can handle himself. The car is what matters.

My fingers are shaking as I open the door, thankful I only need the keys on me for the door to unlock. I press the button and the engine roars to life. *Come on, Caleb!*

He breaks through the trees, two guys still after him. With one push, he sprints ahead. He's not blurring or anything, but he's in seriously good shape. I wonder why he doesn't pour more speed on, unless his amulet still isn't fixed.

I pop open the passenger door so Caleb doesn't have to worry about it.

He slides on the asphalt and swings his way into the car. "Go, go, go!!"

Dude One jumps on the trunk as I shift into gear, the other two following close behind the car. I gun it, probably using a gallon of gas in one go. Dude One is still hanging onto my fender so I swerve until I knock him off. Crap, I really hope he's not hurt, and I'm pretty sure whatever he did to Dad's car is going to get me grounded forever.

"It's okay," Caleb says. "I've dealt with this before. You don't have to worry."

So they are superhuman too. That's a bit of a relief at least. I nod, but I'm still freaked out.

"Your shoes," Caleb says, pointing to my feet.

I smile. We just escaped near death and he's worried about my shoes? "I know, it's okay."

"No. It's not," he argues.

"Look," I say, "let's get home, and then we can worry about this later. I'm sure we can find my shoes again. It's not like everyone is going bushwhacking in that park."

"Okay," he agrees, taking a steadying breath. "You're right."

I don't let my foot off the gas until we're safe at home. It's a good thing there were no police out there or else we'd be in big trouble.

As soon as we're home I'm tempted to try the flight tactic, but Caleb holds me back with a brush of his finger.

"Hey," he softly says when I'm halfway out my door.

More than anything, I want to shower, but if Caleb's going to talk to me...well, I can't really say no to him.

"Hm?" I ask, facing him.

He smiles. Wow, he must not know what a smile can do to a girl. I giggle, but as soon as the sound breaks free I wish I could take it back. My hand flies over my mouth, and a snort squeaks through my nose. That was attractive.

I expect him to be repulsed, but he doesn't look away. Instead, he smiles bigger and leans across the middle console. His finger touches my face, and a hair that was stuck to my lip gloss breaks free.

"You have a leaf," he says, gently pulling it from my locks.

So much for dressing up today.

He's still angled in my direction. Is that all he wanted to talk about? But I don't dare say anything, because the way he's looking at me is causing the bubbles again. Dang, kid doesn't even have to touch me and I'm all screwed up.

"So about my secret," he says, inching closer.

Wow. I've noticed his lips like this before. I mean, I've looked at them plenty. Admired them even. But when they're right in my face...

"You know," he continues, "the parents are probably going to be here soon."

Why is he reminding me of that right now? I don't want to think about it.

"Yeah," I say. It comes out really breathy, but I can't seem to get my body to cooperate with my head. Everything is hazy. All I know is if I inch forward I can make contact with Caleb's lips, but I'm too chicken to do anything about it.

"I was thinking," he says, looking down. It's completely unfair that his lashes are so long and dark when mine require mascara to even show. "If you're okay with it, we—"

"My baby!"

Caleb and I jump back from each other. On the rearview mirror, it shows my dad standing by the car. The minivan idles just behind us. Looks like our parents are back.

"How did this happen?" Dad is sobbing.

I can't get out of the car fast enough. "Dad, I can explain."

"What happened to you?" he says, his voice panicked. "What happened to the car? And your shoes?"

Caleb comes out, too. "It's my fault, Mr. Eom. You see, there was—"

"Blood!" someone screams.

Mrs. Choi is running toward Caleb, her eyes wide. Blood, on Caleb? I guess he's not invincible. He flips around and looks at his shoulder. His shirt is torn and a gash is running down his bicep.

"The tree got me."

Nice excuse. I wonder if he fixed his amulet or not. I was a little busy with Shaun. Maybe he's still getting weaker. As much as I hate to think about him leaving, I wonder if he should go back to Korea so he can get better. We only have three and half days left, anyway.

"It's nothing," he says, shrugging his mom off. "Mr. Eom, I'm so sorry about your car. I'll have it fixed for you."

I step to the back so I can assess the damage. Long, thin nail scratches go all the way down the beautiful racing stripes. Man, that dude had some nails.

"Anna, you're bleeding too," Dad says.

Am I? I didn't notice.

Mom is looking at my torn back. "What happened?" she says, freaking out.

"We got lost in the woods," Caleb says, shooting me a look.

Right, his secret. Good cover.

Caleb turns to my dad again. "I got us stuck, and some branches scraped the car. Then we had to hike, and Anna lost her shoes, and we got hurt."

Dad narrows his eyes as he looks between us. He's not happy, but Caleb sounds so sincere.

"I suppose it can be fixed," he says.

Mom wipes something off my cheek. "You two should go wash up."

Yeah, that shower sounds nice about now.

I nod and start away. The second I pass the front of the car, Caleb is at my side.

"Anna?" Mom calls. I crane my neck to see her. "You can use my bathroom."

Mom! My face must be bright red right now. As if I was going to shower with Caleb.

Caleb's smiling so big it almost reaches his ears. Oh my gosh, this is so bad.

"I'll see you at dinner," Caleb says as we reach our rooms.

Why does that make my stomach boil over?

I guess it's closer to dinner time. Another day where I totally forgot to eat, thanks to the gorgeous guy next to me. Boy, he knows how to turn my world upside down.

"Oh yeah, sure," I say, hoping my voice isn't shaking too much.

He smiles again. "See-ya."

I'm starting to think he was all cold and unfeeling to me because of his secret. Now that he knows I know, he's actually nice. Sweet, even.

I dress in my usual jeans and tee-shirt for dinner, but I don't put makeup on. Too much trouble.

Somehow I don't think Caleb will mind. He's seen me worse, and he was still good to me today. That moment in the bush made me think he's way more than the guy I met at the door a few days ago.

I get to the bottom step and notice Caleb sitting in the living room with Rosie on his lap. Rosie doesn't go to anyone but me. She might be cute and fluffy, but Pomapoos can be seriously picky about who they love.

Celebrity Superhero

My heart squeezes as I watch the two of them. Rosie's little tongue is poking out as she pants leaning into Caleb's touch. Somehow I've forgotten that Caleb is Sungwook and I'm just watching my crush being incredibly adorable with my dog.

I have to watch myself or I might fall for the man in front of me instead of the idol.

# Superheroes Have Feelings, Too

"Good morning," Caleb says to me as I come down the stairs the next day.

It's weird to have him speaking to me so readily, but I don't hate it.

"Morning," I return, feeling shy.

He keeps catching me off guard, totally leaving me defenseless. As if he didn't have an advantage over me.

All the adults are gathered in the kitchen prepping breakfast, and Caleb—still in his pajamas—is sitting in my favorite reading chair with my dog and a book he took off my mom's shelf behind him. He was already so gorgeous, and that book just makes him look more amazing. I wonder what Superman glasses would do to this scene. I have to hold my breath to keep myself from thinking about how much perfection that would be.

"Anna," Mom calls from the kitchen.

Celebrity Superhero

I poke my head in, trying to get Caleb out of my brain, but not succeeding. Mom doesn't turn around, just points to a box on our mail counter. "I think your contacts came."

Yes! I'll finally be able to see again, although my eyes might explode from the beauty that is Caleb.

I grab the box and run back upstairs to put them in. Finally, I can see things how I'm supposed to. The sad part is, I can't imagine Caleb liking me the way I am. *No*, I tell myself, *I will not think that way and ruin my time with him.* If he likes me or not is irrelevant. I like him, and I can keep that to myself for three more days.

After trying to smooth out some fly-aways I turn to notice Caleb's door wide open. The temptation to walk in there and see what he packed is *sooo* enticing, but I'm not a stalker.

I hear his bedroom door click open, and before I can retreat back to my room Caleb is standing in the frame, his back to me as he takes off his pajama shirt.

At first, my feet are glued to the ground, eyes wide.

Seriously, his body on screen is not made up. He really is that ripped. He slides his hands around the edge of his waistband like he's about to take his pants off, but I can't seem to move or look away.

"Stop!" I yell. "I can see you."

Caleb turns around, full smile on his face. I'm surprised my new contacts haven't ripped yet from the way my eyes are bulging.

"Anna," he says in the most casual way, as if he doesn't realize he's a freaking god.

I have no words at all. The most I can hope for is that my drool is contained to the inside of my mouth.

"I wanted to ask you," he continues, coming closer to me.

Yep, his nearness is not helping the speech receptors in my brain. I'm pretty sure he's rendered me a mute. Goodbye talking, I enjoyed you.

He stops right in front of me, one hand leaning on the bathroom counter. All that position has done for him is shown off the amazing muscles in his arms. I can't believe he's the same age as me. He's all man.

"What do you want to do today?"

He keeps talking as if it's easy for me to concentrate on his words. "I think our parents enjoyed some time without us, and you still haven't shown me around Portland."

If I understand right he's asking if we can have more time just the two of us together today, but that wouldn't be logical. I wonder if I'm having delusions now.

"Anna," he says, waving a hand in front of my face. "Hello?"

"I sorry," I croak, finding my voice. "Could you put a shirt on?"

He bites his lip, raising his eyebrows. "What? You can't handle me?"

Crap, why did he have to flex as he said that. That's exactly what's going on, but I can't let him know that.

"Dream on," I say, my wits coming back to me. "It's because you smell. Put some deodorant on while you're at it."

I have to suppress a giggle as he actually smells himself. If only he knew he still smells sweet and chocolaty like he did yesterday, but he already has the upper hand and I'm not going to let him take all the cards.

My brain starts working enough that I'm able to retreat to my room and shut the door, then lean against it. Oh my goodness, he's good at getting to me.

"Anna?" I hear again a few seconds later. "I'm dressed now." I can't answer right away because I'm still recovering. He mumbles. "I put deodorant on, too."

That makes me laugh enough to snap out of it, so I open the door. Okay, that's not any better. Why on earth did he have to put on a white collared shirt with rolled up sleeves? Is he trying to make my disability worse? If he had a tie I'd be a goner.

"I was thinking," he says, pressing his shoulder into the doorframe. "Maybe I can take you out for lunch or a movie or something."

That sounds convincingly like a date.

"You know," he continues, before I can totally think it through. "Since you know my secret, I thought we could talk about it."

Oh, right. I'm just his confidant, not a girl he wants to spend time with. He's trying to get out of me how much I know about his superpowers, but the problem is I'm afraid of divulging too much. If I do, he won't need me anymore, and I'm enjoying being needed.

"Actually," I say, "I think everyone was going to hike Multnomah Falls, and since it's a bit of drive I really want to go with."

He nods, taking a step back from me. "You're right. We should do that instead. I'll just change. Again."

I hate that I can feel the disappointment rolling off him, but I'm getting greedier by the day and I don't really want to lose him.

"I'll meet you downstairs," I say closing the door in his face.

My hand stays on the knob for a second as I try not to curse myself out. It's okay, even if we're going to be hanging around our parents, we'll still be together. Besides, this is what he wanted anyway, to be with his family. I can only imagine the pressures he faces as pop star in Korea. All the groups are worked so hard they hardly have personal time. It must've been really hard for him to come this way.

I don't see Caleb again when Dad tells me to get in the van. He's been packing stuff up all morning like we're camping instead of hiking less than an hour away. As I open the rear door, I notice dad has put one of the seats down so he can lay a bunch of hiking sticks on top. I've done this hike before, and it's not that hard, but I keep my mouth closed since it means Caleb and I will get to sit right next to each other with no space between us.

I take the middle chair as I'm short and skinny and Caleb is taller and more muscular. Just as I imagined his parents sit in the two captain's seats in front and Caleb squishes in next to me. Now he's wearing an athletically fit shirt and shorts. It's obvious he doesn't skip leg day either.

He doesn't say anything to me and looks out the window keeping as far away from me as will allow in the tight space.

"Everything okay?" I ask once we're on the freeway and the parents have their own conversation started.

"I'm fine," he answers, when he is clearly not fine.

I know I hurt him, and I have to make up for it. Pouty Caleb is cute in pictures, but not so much in real life.

"Hey," I say poking his arm. "Don't be a grump. We're stuck in this van for a bit, so we should make the most of it."

"Oh yeah?" he asks, shifting his body so it's facing me. "And how do you plan on making the most of it? It's obvious you don't care about my secret."

Seriously? How could I not care? He's a freaking superhero!

"That's not true," I retort.

He rolls his eyes and turns back to the window.

"The problem is," I say, wanting to make up. I gather all my courage with a deep breath, and gaze at my hands in my lap. "I'm scared."

The words come out in a whisper, but I know Caleb heard them because I can feel him shifting towards me again.

"Hey," he says, lifting my chin and searching my eyes. "You don't have to be afraid of anything. I promise."

"I know," I say with a smile, "but that doesn't make it easier."

He releases my chin and takes my hand instead, causing the heat in my nerves to flame up my stomach again until it reaches a boiling point.

"I know it's complicated," he says, rubbing his thumb along the back of my hand, "but it's not impossible."

I'm starting to think anything is possible with Caleb around, although I don't know what's so difficult about having superpowers. Then again, he must be struggling with his secret identity. Superheroes always seem to have that war within them. He needs my help to keep it under wraps, or else why would he be so tender?

"No matter what," I say in return, "You can depend on me."

I should get over his amazing smile and sparkling eyes by now, but I can't seem to. Each time his face lights up like that I crumble.

He leans down to whisper into my ear. "Tomorrow I'd really like to talk to you in private. Right now, I think our parents are watching us too closely."

His head nods to the front and I see my dad watching us in the rearview mirror, eyebrows knit together. Tomorrow is his last full day here. He won't be leaving until late Sunday night, but it's still not enough time. I guess I can't refuse him then.

Caleb lets go of my hand and goes back to looking out the window. I lace my fingers together and squish them between my legs in an attempt to keep myself from touching him, because right now I want to put my hands all over him.

Multnomah Falls is a place a person could see a thousand times and never get sick of. As the tallest falls in Oregon it would be breathtaking enough, but the quaint fairy bridge in the middle of it adds to the sight.

The falls are famous everywhere around the world, and the bridge is heavily featured each time. I still can't get over it. And the best part of the hike is crossing that very bridge and getting to gaze at the falls close enough to understand the immensity of their power. The only problem is, it's such a neat destination that it's often crowded.

I can tell Caleb is nervous the second we get out of the van. He puts on a hat immediately, keeping the brim low. I feel awful that he has to hide this way when he's such an amazing person. If only everyone could see him like I do.

"It's okay," I say staying right next to him. "If anything happens, I can be a decoy again."

Celebrity Superhero

That makes him laugh enough that he relaxes.

"You're right, there's too many witnesses here for anything bad to happen."

I bump into his shoulder as an excuse to touch him. "Exactly."

Our whole group stops at the bridge, the sound of dumping water making it hard to hear very far. It's enough to have a private conversation, but not talk with the whole group. Caleb and I stay silent as we watch the power of mother nature for a moment, but I'm completely aware of how near he is. The little gab between us is completely charged, the tiniest touch would make it burn.

"Do you remember when," I ask, a sudden nostalgia seizing me. "You wanted to be a witch for Halloween, but your dad wouldn't let you?"

Caleb laughs, throwing his head back as he does. "He made me be a pirate instead. I was only happy because my shirt was almost like a dress, and I wanted to try wearing a skirt once."

I join in his laughter. "I totally remember that, but your dad didn't know you came to my house to play princess dress up with me."

"Oh no," he says pulling his hat brim low. "That's so embarrassing."

I shrug. "It's not. You were four or five, it was cute."

His smile won't quit. "'member the day you wouldn't play with me because I said I liked lemon in my fake tea."

I close my eyes, trying not to let my cheeks heat up, but they do anyway. "No, I had forgotten what a boss I was to you. It *had* to be sugar. Nothing else. You really put up with a lot with me."

He nudges my shoulder so I'm forced to look at him. "No, I didn't," he answers, sounding totally serious. "I loved playing with you. The threat of not playing with you hurt, but I was always worse to you."

I go silent because, yeah, he was. I still can't forgive him for the necklace thing.

"Remember that time," he says, "you and Shaun went for a bike ride without me and I slashed your tires the next day?"

My eyes go wide as I stare at him. I don't remember Shaun in that equation, but I do remember losing my bike. "You slashed my tire? I thought I ran over something."

"I'm so sorry," he says. "I was immature." He looks at the ground and I swear I hear him mumble "and jealous" but I can't be sure because that doesn't sound right and the waterfall is so loud.

"You weren't always awful," I say, a new memory surfacing. "Wasn't there a day at school when my pants ripped and you gave up your over-shirt for me to tie around my waist? I was so mortified and you really saved me. Not many six year olds would think of that."

He still won't look up from the ground. "You know, I wasn't like most six year olds."

I go quiet, wondering how I missed his superpowers when he was younger. I can't imagine the things he went through. It's okay, though. I know now and I'm going to do whatever it takes to help him not have to worry about it anymore.

Caleb and I had plans to hang out the next morning, but our parents managed to wrestle us into spending more time with them at a museum. It's not so bad since they let us go off on our own. Caleb and I continued remembering our childhoods together, which somehow morphed to include all the stuff that happened while we were apart. Expect the whole Idol thing, Caleb still won't mention that.

"Hey," Caleb says the moment we arrive home. "We really need to have that talk tonight."

I nod, knowing I can't avoid it any longer. Tomorrow he's going back to Korea.

"I'll meet you on the back porch after dinner," he says, like it's going to be no big deal.

I decide to change since I dressed up for the museum and it was uncomfortable. I still have no idea what exactly Caleb wants to say, and the suspense is killing me.

The questions he might ask swirled through my brain, leaving me in my own world as I walked down the stairs for dinner, so I didn't notice anyone or anything going on around me.

When I turn the corner, a voice snaps me back to my senses.

"Hey beautiful, you're looking good tonight."

Somehow, Shaun has come for dinner.

# Oh, How the Mighty Fall

I hate to admit it, but Shaun is looking good, too. He's put on new clothes, brand new from the looks of it, and styled his dark hair up and out of his face, all idol-like. It's freaking gorgeous.

"Hey," I say, a little bit of flirt coming out even though I told my mouth not to. What is wrong with me? Wasn't I *just* hating on him a couple days ago? "What are you doing here?"

He rests his back against the wall and curls one leg up, thumbs in his belt loops. His eyes smile as he turns his head my direction. "The Chois invited my family."

Somehow I don't think Caleb was part of that invite, but it's cool. I'm actually glad he's here— it's distracting me from whatever Caleb wanted to say. Not that I don't want to talk to Caleb. I'm more afraid he's going to give me a lecture about keeping his secret, then never speak to me again. That would be the worst.

I shrug. "Well, now you know where I live."

He gives me a half grin. "I still want your number."

Heat rises in my cheeks. No doubt my body has a physical reaction to him. That doesn't mean I have to give into that. Maybe that almost kiss was a mistake, and I misinterpreted his actions. I'll be the bigger person if I give him another shot. I'm still not handing over my number, though. I'm not *that* forgiving.

"Nice try," I say, poking his shoulder as I walk past him and into the main part of the kitchen.

Caleb's violently chopping carrots on the island. I didn't know he could cook. I thought all the bubbles in my tummy had popped after all our time together, but the moment I see Caleb, they start to foam up again. Even though this week's been insane, it's the best time I've had in real life, ever. I haven't been tempted to open a book or turn on my computer once.

Not to mention, what girl doesn't want their own superhero?

I stand opposite him and steal a carrot from his pile. He looks up at me just as I snap off a bite, scrunching my nose.

"That's good," I say with my mouth full.

His knife is still against the orange stalk and his whole face softens as I pop the rest of the slice into my mouth. He shakes his head, mouth bunched up like he's holding back a smile. I wish he wouldn't. I love to see him smile.

I swallow. "You cut that the perfect thickness."

The knife hasn't moved, in fact, he's hardly stirred since he noticed me. I wonder what he's thinking.

I don't let my eyes drop from his gaze, and the longer I look into his eyes, the more lost I become. It's like drowning in a reflection of stars.

"Would you like another?" Shaun says, coming up beside me and holding a carrot to my mouth.

Caleb's shoulders tense again as he continues to chop. I swear he's going to break the cutting board.

Celebrity Superhero

"Thank you," I say, taking a step back and grabbing the carrot out of Shaun's hand.

Caleb glances up, looks between the two of us, and jabs the tip of knife into the wood of the cutting board. Guess he's all out of carrots.

"Anna," Mom says, bustling in. "Will you please set the table?"

I open my mouth to say yes when Shaun chimes in. "I'll help!"

"Me too," Caleb says.

This is a little freaky.

Mom claps her hands together, beaming. "Such nice boys."

She opens a drawer and pulls out the placemats. "For you," she says, putting the stack in Caleb's arms. Plates come out next. "And for you," she says, loading Shaun up.

I get stuck with the silverware. Why do I have a feeling that's a bad omen?

We shuffle to the formal dining room, where an eerie silence takes over after the din of boiling water and slicing knives.

Caleb sets down his first placemat. "Anna, you should do the silverware next."

"That doesn't make any sense," Shaun says, an edge to his voice. "Look," he continues. "I have to put down the plate so she can know how to space the silverware."

Caleb slaps down his stack of placemats. "Fine, you take over these, and I'll do the plates."

"Not a chance," Shaun retorts, "I was entrusted these plates by Anna's mother. It's my duty to hand them out."

Caleb looks like he's about to rip the placemats apart. I don't get what's making him so mad.

I set down the silverware and ease the wicker mats from Caleb's hands. "I'll just do this."

Caleb blinks and rips the mats back. "No thank you." He grabs the silverware as well, or part of it anyway. "I think they need more help in the kitchen."

To me, it looked like there were more people in the kitchen than there needed to be, but I'm not going to say that. It's clear Caleb wants me out of the room. He's probably mad at Shaun for something. My superhero collation suspicion is fading.

Celebrity Superhero

Maybe Shaun is his arch nemesis. We were attacked right after we went to his house. There's that phrase, 'keep your friends close and your enemies closer.' Seems like that's what Caleb's doing. Although, I'm not sure why Shaun would help Caleb get his powers back. Unless he likes a challenge.

Or maybe I'm taking this whole thing a step too far. I look back in the room to see the boys laughing. The truth is, Caleb probably didn't want me around now that his friend is here. He was probably only nice to me when we were alone. Can't say that doesn't hurt me, but I'll get over it. I think.

Since the main dining table only seats six adults and Shaun's parents are here, Caleb, Shaun, and I are all at small round kids table shoved in the corner. I feel a little squished as both boys move their chairs closer to me.

I wonder if they want me to leave again. I'm getting in the middle of their bro time. I shovel in my kimchi and rice, ignoring the conversation around me. Geez, it's hot in here.

"Can someone please pass me more bulgogi?" I say, mouth full.

I didn't notice until now that the table is silent. Both boys are staring at me. Did I do something wrong?

I swallow, one hard lump of rice sticking in my throat. "What?"

"You didn't hear my question?" Shaun asks.

I take a sip of water to help with the rice and it ends up going down the wrong tube. My eyes water as I cough. "Sorry," I squeak. "What was that?"

Shaun puts his arm around the back of my chair. "I was asking what school you go to. I know it's summer, but I'm still curious."

I regain my composure and dab my mouth with a napkin. "Lincoln." Not that there's anything exciting about that.

"Well, my school has an exchange program," Shaun says, smiling.

Like, foreign exchange? Doesn't every school have that? "Cool."

He twirls his chopsticks over his knuckles. *Show off.* "So you'll go to school with me?"

Wait, did I miss something? Why would I go to his school?

"Seriously?" Caleb asks, his chopsticks held in his knuckles like a weapon.

"Uh." I tuck my hair behind my ear. "Can I go to your school?"

"Yeah." Shaun laughs. "It's an exchange program, so you come to my school, and then I see what you do for a day."

Oh, that kind of exchange.

"Maybe?" I answer, feeling uneasy.

"Let me get this straight," Caleb says, his chopsticks almost drilling a hole through his plate. "You spend two whole days together?"

What is Caleb's deal? I swear I have no idea what he's thinking from one second to the next.

Shaun is still twirling his chopsticks and I want to rip them out of his hand. "Yeah, it's a local thing. Better way to get to know the people who *live* here."

The way Shaun said *live* sends chills down my spine, and not in a pleasant way. It's almost like he's rubbing his residence in Caleb's face.

"I don't have to leave, you know," Caleb says, confirming my theory.

But that wouldn't be good. He has his career back in Korea. In fact, considering the latest MV release, I'm surprised he's not starting a tour right away.

"No, you can't," Shaun says. It's a statement of fact; everyone who knows K-pop knows Caleb's tied down by his contract. "Besides," Shaun adds, "Don't you want Anna to be happy?"

Whoa. This conversation is taking a massive turn. I'm not sure why Caleb staying or going has anything to do with me.

Caleb's fist loosens, just a touch. "Yeah, I do."

My head hurts. It's like my brain has moved to half speed and I'm ten steps behind this conversation. Caleb wants me to be happy. That's new.

"Exactly," Shaun says, "I'm the one who can be here."

Celebrity Superhero

Has the world fallen off its axis or something? Everything is spinning sideways and my mind cannot connect.

Caleb drops his chopsticks and spreads out his fingers until his palms are flat against the table. His head bows as his back curls. "You're right. I'm glad for you two."

So. Dang. Lost.

Unless... What if those attackers earlier today are now after me and this conversation is about keeping me safe? So the superhero collation thing was right. Glad to know Shaun's not an enemy.

Actually, I'm glad Shaun is here to protect me. I hadn't considered what it might mean once Caleb left.

After dinner, the three of us go into the living room to chat. I sit on the couch and Shaun takes his place next to me. Really close to me, again. But if Caleb believes in Shaun, I do too. Plus, there's the whole hotness thing.

I take one look at Caleb who's sitting in my usual reading chair on the other side of the room. Rosie takes one look at him, then comes over and hops on my lap. She yips once at Shaun then curls up on legs with her butt facing him. That's the Rosie I know.

Caleb's not looking at me. He's been an ice prince since Shaun got here, so I shouldn't be surprised. Although, the way he's glancing out the window all dejected makes me think it's more than him being moody.

"So," Shaun says, drawing my attention back to him.

He smells like sweet lemon. It's super yummy.

His eyes are such a clear brown, I feel like I can see right through them. Brilliant, vibrant, beautiful.

"Can I have your number now?"

My eyes flick to Caleb again. I don't know why I feel like I need his approval, but I do.

He hinted that it was okay. Also, it'll be nice to have someone who knows Caleb to commiserate with when Caleb leaves.

"Fine," I say, "but only if you promise to use it well."

Shaun slings an arm behind my shoulders. "Oh, I will."

Gosh, Shaun is smooth. I find myself looking at Shaun's lips, wondering how close he's going to get before he stops. I won't let him kiss me, my parents are in the next room, even if they're not paying attention. Caleb too. Who's *also* not paying attention.

Shaun adjusts, moving the hand that was behind my back to the side of my ear like he's going to tell me a secret. "I'd really like to take you out on a date. How about it?"

Wait, since when did his protection include dating? I'm sure my face is bright red judging by the flush I feel in my cheeks. Goodness, he's direct.

Someone takes my hand and pulls me off the couch. Caleb's face is red. "We need to talk, now."

What the frack? Seriously, does Caleb think I'm going to blab to Shaun about his powers? I don't see why it matters, but there's nothing else that would make him this mad. I feel like I've been jerked around ever since Shaun arrived and

I'm sick of it. I was just starting to forget about how sucky it's going to be when Caleb leaves.

I wrench my arm out of his grip. "What is your deal tonight? We can talk later."

His hands ball at his sides, nostrils flaring. When he looks at me, his eyes are glassy with water. "Please. Just for a minute."

There has to be something more happening here. I thought this was what he wanted for me. To be happy. I was just trying to do that. Obviously, we do need to talk. I guess Shaun will still be here later.

I give Shaun a smile. "I'll be right back."

Caleb stomps ahead of me out to the back deck. A light rain pelts my head, mist rising off the ground. Caleb starts pacing, his fists clenching again. I swear he's going to punch something.

He flips around at me, and I stumble backward. "I thought you said you knew my secret."

I swallow, hands shaking. "I do."

He pulls at his hair until it's all messed up. Why does he have to do things that are so dang cute when I'm trying to get over him? "Then why are you doing this? Does it really matter if I can't stay?"

It doesn't matter, of course it doesn't. I'll still keep his secret.

"My lips aren't that loose," I say, shaking my head. "But I don't get it. How do my actions have any effect on your secret?"

Caleb starts laughing—throwing his head back, and clutching his stomach.

Okay, I wasn't expecting that reaction. I don't see what's so funny.

"Let me ask you this," he says once he's gained a hint of composure. "What do you think my secret is?"

I shuffle my feet. It feels weird to say it, but it's not like he doesn't know what he's capable of. "I know about your superpowers," I answer, point blank. "Speed, excellent hearing, extended sight. It was pretty obvious."

Caleb's jaw drops open, one eyebrow cocked.

"You're part of SUPER, and your powers are real," I continue, but I'm starting to doubt myself.

That has to be his secret. He can't have any other secrets. Why do I feel like he has other secrets?

I lightly punch his shoulder. "Come on, what else can you do?"

He screams a laugh, and then doubles over slapping his knee. If I thought he was crazy before, he looks downright insane now. He's laughing so hard I'm worried it's going to hurt him.

He looks up at me, wipes a tear, and then starts laughing again. He's gasping for breath, curled into himself as his body shakes. "You...you thought..."

He snorts, slapping his knee again.

Now my head is ready to crack open. It hurts to think about his reactions. The only thing I know is that I must've done something wrong.

Caleb grips my shoulder, trying to keep a straight face. "Anna, I don't have superpowers."

No. I've witnessed it. I mean, how else could he have done all those things?

I cross my arms. "You don't have to pretend around me. You caught the vase, and you heard my bowl break. Then you saw that bird—"

He shudders. "Don't talk about birds. They terrify me."

He can't change the subject, I need answers. "Then there were those thugs that were trying to kill you."

Both his eyebrows shoot up. "Trying to kill me? Really?"

This doesn't make any sense. Why doesn't this not make any sense?

"You just said yourself that I'm part of SUPER," Caleb says, lifting his chin. "If you know that, you know there are some crazy fans who always find me and try stuff. They even followed me here from Korea to try and get close to me. They're nuts. My group members told me they've set up camp at Forest Park since they saw me there once. That's how crazy they are."

The dots still aren't connecting. He has to know he can't hide his powers from me. More than that, I need to *not* be insane. "Look," I start, "I know all about sasaeng fans. I mean, I'm

Korean. It's kinda hard for me to avoid. But that still doesn't explain everything I saw."

Caleb is looking at the ground, his lovely black hair falling in his face. When he speaks, his voice sounds dejected. "You wanna know, huh? Well, the day I arrived, I was already coming toward you when the vase dropped. As for the bowl, everyone heard it cracking, you were just in your own world. And that bird, well, I do have good vision, but I also noticed because I was freaked out."

Everything in me wants to scream that he's a liar. Everything but my heart. The thought starts there then pumps through my veins until my brain finally gets it. Caleb really doesn't have powers. All the crap that's happened around me was just made up. My imagination has blinded me from the truth.

So that was it then. He wasn't immortal. He didn't have superpowers. It actually makes more sense when I consider it. Heck, he was even bleeding after we ran from his fans.

Celebrity Superhero

One more question. If he can answer this, then I'll know. "I guess that jewelry you were talking about isn't an amulet of power then?"

Caleb is sober now, all the laughter drained from earlier. "No. I don't know where you got that idea, but I'm human. One hundred percent."

I want to cry. I feel so stupid. How could I have let myself get this caught up in my own world? I knew I was daydreamer, but this...it's too much. I wouldn't be surprised if Caleb never wants to speak to me again.

The drops that were pattering before turn from a mist to a full-on downpour, soaking my hair and dripping down my face.

"Anna, I—"

"Don't," I say, I can't hear it. Can't even think about all the idiotic things I've done. Caleb has to hate me for these past two days. I've been nothing but a pest.

I have to go. I can't stay here and look into his dark, sparkly eyes and feel like a person that deserves to be in his presence. Something has to be done.

My head shakes as I take two slow steps back. Caleb can't grab me now. I won't let him get near me until I figure this out.

That's when I run inside. I don't take my wet shoes off at the back door. Mom will scold me later, but it doesn't matter. My legs feel like weights as I climb the stairs and slam the door to my room.

Stupid, blind, ignorant, and above all, selfish. A manga sits on my bed, and I can't stand the sight of it. It's these alternate worlds that have gotten me here. My stupid daydreaming has made me totally incompetent to the people around me.

My hand trembles as I pick up the book. At first I think of throwing it in the trash, but I know I'll go back and get it later if it's still intact. If I'm going to do this thing for real, I have to do it all the way.

The spine creaks as I open to the middle. My eyes catch some of the words—it's the first kiss, my favorite part of this book. I sniff, nostrils flaring. I will not cry and I won't let this go on any longer.

Celebrity Superhero

As the page rips from the book, so does my heart. I shred it so thoroughly, it's nothing but confetti on the ground. With each paper that scratches away from the spine, blood pours from inside my chest.

It's all over.

There's a knock on the door, but it's not the door from the hall, it's the door to the bathroom.

"Anna?"

I can't talk to Caleb right now. I crumple to the ground and try to pick up the shreds of my book, but the stupid tears are blocking my vision.

"I'm sorry I laughed," Caleb says. "You just surprised me."

Surprised? Oh, he's being so nice right now. If I were in his shoes, I would hate me. I do hate me.

"But look," he continues despite my silence. "There's something I want to give you—"

Everything is messed up. So messed up I need time to sort through it all. "Just go away," I shout. "I want to be alone right now."

There's a rustle on the other side of the door, and when Caleb speaks again, it sounds like he's sitting. "Glad to know you're in there, and that you're listening to me."

My head falls into my hands. I'm not sure why he's sticking around especially when I've been such a dummy. I stay silent, waiting for him to give up. It's quiet for so long I'm almost convinced he's left, but I know I'd at least hear his door closing.

"Listen," he says. "It stopped raining."

I listen. The silence is eerie. Doesn't stop me from keeping my mouth closed, though.

Caleb inhales loud enough for me to hear. "I'm starting to feel like when I talk to you, I never say what I really want."

Whoa, where did that come from? What could he want to say to me after everything I've done to him?

This very moment I'm considering a career as professional loser. I already have all the qualifications.

"So, maybe we can start over." He clears his throat. "Hi, I'm Caleb," he says, his voice smiling. "We were kids together." He sighs, and I hear the back of his head hitting the door again. "I don't know if you remember, but one time you dared to me to climb a tree. I made it up three branches and you scaled it to the top. After we got down, I threw a water balloon at you as hard as I could. I only did that because I thought you were pretty cool."

I vaguely remember that day. How did that one slip through all the memories? I sniff a laugh.

Caleb laughs too. "Glad you're still there. I'm sorry about that."

Ugh, my cheeks are all wet and my eyes hurt. I swipe at my face. "You don't have to do that, you know," I say. My voice is all scratchy.

When he speaks, it's quieter. "Do what?"

As if he doesn't know. Every girl who's seen him perform has fallen fast and hard. He can sing, dance, act, and he has amazing chocolate abs. There's no reason he should be nice to me. He shouldn't be giving me the time of day.

"Be nice," I say, scolding him. "It's okay. You were forced here."

134

"Anna—"

"No, seriously. Just don't. It's easier that way. I'm going to bed now."

I stand up, brushing the paper from the ripped book off my lap. I'll clean it up in the morning. The only problem is, I really need to brush my teeth, take out my contacts, and go to the bathroom. I get in my pajamas anyway, climb under the covers and turn out the light. If I can pretend to be in bed, then maybe he'll get the hint and leave.

"Anna," he says again after I'm snuggled in and quiet. "Don't you want to know what my secret is?"

# BECOMING A HERO

Holy Hanna. What does he think I am, a robot? Of course I want to know what his secret is. My body is shaking just thinking about it. But I made myself a promise when I walked into the room, a promise that I wouldn't get caught up. This is reality. Secrets, they're nothing but trouble. They're the reason I'm lying here, doing the potty dance and wishing Caleb would leave the bathroom.

He knows I'm not asleep. No one falls asleep that fast. Which means, if I'm ever going to brush my teeth, I have to hurt him.

"No, I don't. I'm not even curious."

I listen as Caleb stands. "I guess that's it then. Goodnight, Anna. Sleep well."

Yeah right. I'm not getting a lick of shut-eye tonight. I wait until his side of the door closes, and then I wait a little longer.

Hopping isn't a strong enough term for the way I spring out of bed and make it to the toilet.

136

I sure hope Caleb isn't listening in because there's a freaking waterfall pouring out of me right now. It's pretty embarrassing, but I don't think it'll make a difference at this point.

After going through my bedtime routine, I lie back in bed. I don't know why though, because memories from the day are pounding, pounding, pounding through my head.

I try to make them go away, but every time I do, Caleb's smile keeps appearing behind my eyelids. Smiling when I tried aegyo. Smiling in the bush. Smiling as we remembered together.

I whip the covers off and stand. Obviously, I cannot live with my mind right now. I need something to distract me. Normally in this situation I'd grab a book off the shelf or watch some K-pop, but I can't do that anymore.

What do regular people do when they need an escape? I don't have the slightest clue. I've been so far from regular I thought a normal human boy had superpowers.

The computer is too much of a temptation— it holds all my fantasies, and I know the second I touch it, I'll give in. What was there before computers? Before books, even?

Cavemen. That's what there was. And they spent most of their time surviving. They also lived in caves. The great outdoors. I grab my glasses, tip open a curtain, and look out.

Fog creeps along the ground, its gray wisps searching for more moisture as it floats on errant winds.

A slice of yellow light cuts through the grass in front of the back door and a shadow stands in the pool of illumination. A shadow that looks just like Caleb. Rosie is sitting at his side, her puffy tail wagging.

The door closes so only the dim blue glow of the porch light is visible. Caleb is stock still. I can't see his face so I have no idea what he's thinking. He just stands, as immovable as the wooden fence next to him.

Yeah, the great outdoors suck too. I should turn away. I should try to sleep. I should do everything I can to get Caleb out of my head, but I don't. Instead, my fingers touch the cool glass, condensation pooling around my hand.

My palm presses into the window. This week was the first time in a long while that I've felt alive. With one stupid thought, I've thrown any semblance of life in the trash.

Truth is, my life is standing under my window, holding so still he becomes part of the landscape.

That's when he screams. Actually, it's more like a roar. A guttural sound ripping from his throat into the dead night air.

Nothing moves but his head, which tilts up to the sky. Pain. Even though I can't see his face, I know it's pain. The same pain I'm feeling.

Could it be...? I don't dare hope, but if he's feeling the same pain then maybe that pain is because of me.

I rush down the stairs, flinging open the back door. "Caleb!" I say, out of breath, but he's not there.

What the—? He was just here. I saw him through my window. I'm sure it was him. There's no way he could've gotten upstairs and past me. It's things like this that make me confused about whether he's superhuman or not.

Celebrity Superhero

A high-pitched scream pierces the night, definitely something from a girl. A muffled "Anna!" in Caleb's voice follows a second later.

I run to the side of the house and peek around the fence. The garage light has flipped on and a giant white van sits in the back driveway. People clad in black, probably the same he fought earlier, drag Caleb into the wide open backend of the vehicle. Sasaeng fans, no doubt. If it wasn't for motion sensor light that turned on, I wouldn't have seen them at all.

Blood drips down the arm of one of his captors. I hope he hurt her.

Instinct begs me to move, to get right in-between these so-called-fans and Caleb, but I know it's not going to work. I tried that earlier today and got myself hurt. This time I have to be smart.

All the kidnappers pile in the van but don't leave right away. The engine starts to rumble, but they still don't go. Is Caleb fighting them? I really wish he *did* have superpowers.

The craziest idea I've ever had pops into my head. Okay, maybe not the craziest, but something that's so out there I don't know if I dare do it. The van has double doors that open in the back, with handles that stick out to grab onto the vehicle.

After another second of indecision, the van starts to inch forward, lights off. It's now or never. No matter what, I have to save Caleb.

Once again, I'm confronted with fight or flight. Everything in me is screaming to run the other direction and call the police to handle this instead, but I don't give in. My legs pump, the wet grass slick under my already cut-up bare feet. I don't care if I fall, I'll get up.

On the street, pebbles rip into my soles. I don't care, I don't care, I do *not* care.

My fingers graze the back of the van as it picks up speed. I pump harder, begging my body to keep moving. I latch one hand onto the bumper and the other onto the handle.

One pull is all I need to get my foot up to the bumper, but the second I pull, the door to opens. Why didn't these crazies lock the van? Anyone could hop in.

Celebrity Superhero

Fear escapes in the form of a gasp as the door bursts me backward, my only grip on the handle that opened the door. Now I'm hanging on parallel to the van and so low my toes scrape the ground. It's enough pain to make my eyes are water.

I swing my free arm around, trying to catch the inside handle so I can pull myself up. Metal scrapes under my fingernails, and I'm flying once again.

The van picks up speed, and since I have very little upper body strength, my fingers begin to slip one by one.

Must. Save. Caleb.

I flip my free arm around again, and this time I grab the handle.

Must. Save. Caleb.

His kidnappers found a broomstick and they use to try and push my hand off the inside of the van.

MUST SAVE CALEB.

I move the hand that was on the outside of the door to the inside, leaving my elbow free to knock the broom away. The door begins to swing shut and I decide to use the momentum to raise feet and knock over the nearest kidnapper.

The push against the kidnapper's body keeps the door from closing all the way, and my pajama pant hooks onto the divider between the doors near my knee. My hands slip, causing the door to fly back to its parallel position. Now I'm hanging out the rear, even with the ground, my stuck pajamas the only thing keeping me in place. Luckily I had gotten far enough into the van that I don't fall out, but my back arches with my head dangerously close to the asphalt.

Hands are touching my knee, trying to set me free, but I can't let that happen. I'll die. I do the most glorious sit-up of my life and slap the sasaeng away.

"Soon Mi-ah!" someone yells. The van skids to a stop, the door swinging shut on my side. I gasp, but do not give up.

MUST SAVE CALEB.

The van takes off again, stretching my body to a breaking point and re-opening the van door. I don't know how much longer my pants can hold the weight.

Celebrity Superhero

The hands are back at my knee when it happens, fabric ripping all the way down my calf and rocking me free.

I'm thrown to the street as I *roll, roll, roll* across the unforgiving blacktop.

Dirt sticks to my palms, blood running down my leg. I try to stand, but the pain is too great. I couldn't win.

When Caleb needed me the most, I let him go.

I'll never forgive myself.

I should've been more careful, I should've never let Caleb out of my sight. He told me people were here trying to mess with him, but he let his guard down. I'm pretty sure it's my fault since I was the last person he spoke to. And I couldn't even save him.

If I had really been smart, I would've taken down the license plate number and called the police like my instinct begged, but I had to be stupid and try to play the part of the hero. I guess I still haven't learned how to live in the real world.

Bright headlights sting my eyes. I raise a hand to shield my face as the car rolls to a stop in front of me. The driver's door opens and a shadowy figure says, "Anna?"

I blink as the figure runs to my side and touches my shoulders. Shaun.

"What happened? Are you okay?" he asks, frantically searching me. "Your leg!"

I push him off, still in shock over losing Caleb. "What are you doing here?"

He shakes his head. "Let's get you safe first, and bandage that leg up. Can you walk?"

I nod, but still stumble when I try to stand. He takes my arm and drapes it around his shoulders. I manage to put some weight on my foot with his help and he sits me in the passenger seat but doesn't put my legs inside. He reaches over me to the glove box and pulls out a first aid kit. Everything in me is numb. The whole incident a blur. I know I should do something, anything, to find Caleb but it's like the gears in my brain can't connect so nothing moves.

Shaun tenderly takes my foot and starts to wrap it.

"I went home," he says, like he's trying to get something off his chest. "But honestly, I couldn't stop thinking about you. You ran upstairs so suddenly, I was worried. When I came back and went to your room, you were gone, and Caleb was missing too. Your whole family is out looking for you."

All of my pent-up frustration releases in the form of tears. The reminder that I'm not the only one who cares for Caleb makes what happened really real and I'm so scared. "We have to go save him," I say between sobs.

Shaun finishes wrapping my leg, but I can still feel him at my feet. I peek through my fingers and see him watching me. "Save who?" he asks.

I want to answer, but the tears are coming so hard and fast I'm having a hard time catching my breath.

He stands, patting my back and cooing, "It's okay." But it's not.

"We have to get them," I say attempting to explain again.

Shaun crouches down to examine my injury again. I can't figure out why he's not as panicked as I feel, but he doesn't know what happened to Caleb, and he was looking for *me*, not him.

"I don't think it's broken," he says, turning my leg. The pain in my leg has dulled, but my side is still throbbing. "It's just a big cut. I think I can get you home now."

"No!" I cry, managing to get my emotions together with a few sniffles. I put my own legs in the car and buckle up. "Caleb's in danger."

I'm still not sure he believes me, but I shut the door in his face and he's forced to take the driver's seat.

He gives me a gentle smile as he puts the car into drive. "You're the one who's hurt. I'm sure Caleb can take care of himself."

I throw the car in neutral so he can't go. He doesn't get it. He has no idea what went down. "Caleb's been kidnapped. We have to save him."

Shaun squeezes his eyes shut and shakes his head like he's trying to clear something from his brain. "Hang on a second. Is that why your leg is hurt? You did that for him?"

"Please," I beg, willing him to understand the situation. "Let me save him."

Shaun leans into the headrest and bangs the steering wheel. "You like *him*, don't you?"

Seriously? Caleb's life is in danger. "Is that important?"

Shaun looks at me, dark hair falling in his face. "No," he says quietly. "It's not, it's just that I'm a little pre-occupied by you."

I can't believe this is happening right now. Each second we lose, Caleb's in further danger. But I need Shaun's help. I can't do this on my own.

"Shaun," I say, putting on my commanding voice. "If it came down to a choice between the two of you, I would chose him." It surprises me how fast it comes out of my mouth, but I'm sure.

For the first time in my life, I know there's only one person for me: Caleb. Whether or not he's here, no one else can replace him. It stinks because I don't know what the future holds. It could mean I'm single forever, but I'm not that upset. All I want is for Caleb to be happy, with or without me. "It's not that I don't like you," I say to Shaun, "if we had met any other way—"

"I get it," he says. "You picked him back then, and you're picking him again."

What is he talking about? "Back then?"

"It's not important." He eases my hand off the shifter. "You told me the truth, so I'll help you. Where do think Caleb is?"

We've been stopped in the middle of the street for so long, I'm sure there's no way we could follow them. Luckily, this street isn't busy and no one's out tonight.

"I don't know," I confess squeezing my eyes close. "The other day they attacked us at the park."

I sit straighter, a shot of energy returning to me. "Forest Park!" I shout. "Caleb said they had set up camp there."

He nods. "Forest Park it is. We should call the police before we go." He flips open the glove compartment and points at a white box. "You should take some painkillers, I have a feeling you're going to need it."

Celebrity Superhero

"Good idea."

Shaun briefs 911 on the situation as we head to save Caleb. Then he calls my parents to tell them I'm safe and we'll only be gone for a little while. I'm glad he lied to them. I have to see Caleb for myself. There's no way I can go home. Shaun is driving like a madman, but it's not fast enough. I twist my hands and bounce in my seat.

"Calm down," Shaun says, "Caleb is my friend, I want him to be safe too."

My head goes up and down fast, but my un-injured leg is still shaking.

Shaun clicks the radio on, and I see his phone is hooked up to an aux port. He must think a little music will help. Nine times out of ten, I'd agree. But not today. Because the first song playing is *Earth Shatter*.

I slap the music off. "I'm sorry," I say, "I just can't."

Shaun picks up his phone. "I didn't know that was on. Let me find something else."

He changes it to something instrumental. It helps, but not much. I'm still worried.

As we approach the park, Shaun turns off his lights. Sure enough, the big van is in the parking lot. At least we're in the right place.

"Stay here," Shaun says, flinging back his seatbelt but leaving the keys in the ignition.

Fat chance of that. I take the keys out and wait until Shaun's figure is nothing more than an outline against the inky night.

The first step out of the car is the hardest. I grit my teeth as I put weight on my leg. The painkillers are helping, but I still feel the gash and the pain in my side. That's not going to stop me. Caleb is more important.

There are voices ahead of me, Shaun arguing something I can't quite hear. I keep my distance, hiding behind a giant tree trunk.

There's a floodlight attached to the ranger shed, illuminating all the open ground in front. I draw closer. Shaun has his arms folded and he's telling the girl standing out front how much trouble she's in.

"Just give up now," he says.

The girl is trembling, but she doesn't move. "I don't know if I can do that."

Why are these people doing this? Shaun is telling them how sick it all is, and they still don't budge. I just hope they don't hurt Caleb before I can save him.

"What is this?" some lady says, barging out of the ranger shed. She's tall, thin, and really beautiful. Even though I don't see well in the dark, I can tell. She also looks like she's in charge.

"I...I...I..." the trembling girl answers

Shaun faces the lady. "Look, Caleb is my best friend. Can I just talk to him?"

Beautiful Lady stands for a minute looking Shaun over. Her hands are shoved in the pockets of a stylish trench coat. "No," she says simply, pulling out a black box from her pocket.

I want to scream, but I hold it in. Shaun's whole body convulses as she shoves the black box—a taser—against Shaun's arm. Shaun crumples to the ground, passing out.

There has to be a way to stop these lunatics.

"That's it, Soon Mi," the trembling girl says in Korean. "I'm not doing this anymore. This isn't a mission to save SUPER like you told me. You just tasered that guy."

Soon Mi sighs loudly, whips the taser around and stuns her friend in the arm, causing her to collapse.

Holy crap. This just got ten times more serious. How can I save Caleb with an injury and zero fighting skills? She's ruthless. I bet she doesn't care who gets in her way.

She proves my thoughts correct by tying Shaun and the girl together and dragging them to the side of the shed.

I have to be smart. Way smarter than I was earlier. It's clear Soon Mi's intent is to harm, not help.

My mind wanders to all the manga I've read. I add in *The Avengers*, *Batman*, *Wonder Woman*, and just about every other action movie I can think of. One line that's common in most movies keeps playing in my head.

What I need is a distraction.

There's only one thing I can think of that would distract a K-pop fan from her idol—more K-pop.

Celebrity Superhero

I run/limp back to Shaun's car and get in the driver's seat. This is so crazy, and I'm probably going to get killed. I have to do it though, Caleb means that much to me. I can't let him go.

The engine purrs to life. I bite my tongue as I hit the gas, trying to push past the pain in my right leg. I gun it enough to get over the sidewalk curve, spinning the wheels in the soft dirt under the grass.

For Caleb's sake, I pray the car doesn't get stuck until I can be in front of the ranger shed.

I park a safe distance from the building, safe enough I won't get tased.

For a moment, I consider just ramming the car into Soon Mi who's standing outside looking straight into the headlights. But I could lose control and hit other people, including Shaun. Plus, that might get me some jail time, and I'm not that careless.

My hands shake as I pick up Shaun's phone. Soon Mi is looking at me, but she's not moving closer. Okay, I hope I can do this.

Just as I thought, Shaun has all of SUPER's songs. I turn his stereo up full blast—bass shaking the windows. I flip open the passenger door and then step out the driver's side, leaving the door open for the sound to leak out. Caleb's singing voice fills the air as I step in front of the car.

Unique picks up singing next, and I start to do the dance. My moves are sloppy because of my injuries, but I'm doing the best I can and the painkillers have fully kicked in. It gets to the chorus and Soon Mi's arms relax. She's starting to mirror my movements, but only slightly.

Pain screams through my nerves as I do a little twist on the ground, but I don't stop. A few other captors come out of the shed to see what's going on. They all start dancing too—the fangirl mood infectious.

I know how K-pop fans are. When they get the chance to enjoy it, they enjoy it all the way. Especially crazy obsessed fans who would kidnap their idol.

I slowly dance my way forward, and many of the girls dance their way towards me.

Finally, Caleb's slow high note comes, and Soon Mi gets totally lost in the music. From her movements, I can see how much she admires Caleb. That's when I realize, she's wearing my shoes. It's all in now.

I end up dancing my way behind her. The other girls crowd around starting to form a circle. I take the moment of chaos and slip into the shed. I barely reach Caleb before the next song on the album starts blasting out of Shaun's car.

Caleb's eyes widen as he sees me. He's tied to a chair, mouth taped, huddled in a smelly corner.

"I'm sorry," I say as I rip the adhesive off his lips.

"You shouldn't be here," he replies in a frantic whisper. "I saw what you did when they took me."

"Shhh." I try to untie his hands.

The door slams open, Soon Mi looming in the sickly-yellow light. The other girls are still dancing outside and having a good time.

I scramble faster to untie him, but Soon Mi hits me across the side of my head and I stumble back.

"No!" Caleb screams.

I force myself to stand, putting all the pressure on my good leg.

Soon Mi's sitting on Caleb's lap, sealing his mouth with more duct tape.

Not on my watch. Time to make like a rhino and charge.

Pain? I don't know what pain is, all I know is speed. My head makes contact with Soon Mi's side, and I knock over Caleb's chair as well.

I read somewhere that the elbow is the strongest part of the body, so I try to jab at Soon Mi's jaw. She rolls on top of me, pulling my hair.

A primal roar bellows from my mouth as I grab hold of her head. We're rolling around on the floor, Soon Mi trying to kick me. As soon as I'm on top, I sit on Soon Mi's torso. She lets go of my hair long enough to slap my cheek.

I'm thrown off balance and we switch positions. She yanks my hands out of her hair and pins them to the ground. Then she sits on them so I'm completely stuck.

"Nice try, Princess," Soon Mi says, "But you're never getting him back. He's mine."

I wriggle the best I can, but it's no use. Soon Mi's hand is in her pocket, no doubt she's trying to pull out the taser. I flick my eyes in Caleb's direction, but he's not in the chair anymore. He's not in the chair anymore! I must have loosened his ties just enough.

"We'll see about that," Caleb says, hitting Soon Mi in the side of the head with a two-by-four. She falls sideways, releasing me, but I can still see her breathing. She looks okay, too, just unconscious.

We did it, we're saved. K-pop saved us. I want to reach out to Caleb but all the adrenaline has drained out, leaving me weak.

"Shaun," I say, remembering. "We have to help him. He got me here, risked himself."

But we can't leave yet, not with the other girls still dancing outside.

Caleb gathers me in his arms and presses me to his chest. "Are you okay? Where are you hurt?"

I'm so stunned I don't hug him back.

"I'm fine," I say, even though it's a lie. "Are you okay?"

He leans away so he can get a better look at me. "I'm great as long as you are."

The look in his eye snaps me back to reality. A reality where I've messed things up with Caleb and he'll never like me the way I like him. I try to push him, but he pulls me back in his arms, his face buried in my hair.

"I'm fine, really," I say again. It's hard to think.

My brain isn't processing the way Caleb's hands are gripping me, how tight he's holding my waist, like he needs me. I'm just glad he's alive.

Caleb moves his hands from my hips to my chin. "After what happened at the van, I thought I lost you. I can't go another second without telling you—"

"Come out with your hands up," an officer says over a megaphone.

Red and blue lights flash outside the door. The police are here. Now we're really saved.

"It can wait," I tell him. I don't want it to wait, but I need a minute to pull myself together anyway.

Celebrity Superhero

He swallows. "Okay, but I'm not letting you go."

# The Good Guy Always Wins

My parents are so freaked out they won't let me sleep in my room. All six of us—me, Caleb, my parents, and his parents—are camping out in the living room. That's fine with me because Caleb literally will not let go. There hasn't been a moment where he's not touching me since it all ended.

Even as we lie down to sleep, he holds me tight around my ribs, only our sleeping bags keeping us apart.

"Can you believe that girl wanted to keep you as her puppet?" I say for the umpteenth time.

Our parents are already sleeping, Caleb and I whispering in the dark.

"I know," he responds, "and she told everyone helping her she had a plan to make SUPER even better. I can't believe they all followed her."

It's more nuts than me, no matter which way I look at it. "I'm just glad no one got overly hurt."

161

"Especially you," Caleb says, snuggling his nose into my neck.

This doesn't feel real. Caleb is holding me, really holding me. I giggle. "Seriously, I was really worried about Shaun too."

Caleb releases his hold, resting his head on one fist so he can see me better. He keeps his other arm draped around me. I turn to lie on my back so I can see him too.

"Really?" he says, "You're going to bring Shaun into this?"

A smile raises the corner of my mouth. "Why? Are you jealous?" I'm teasing, wondering if my hopes are real.

Caleb looks serious. "Uh, yeah."

There's no way this is happening. It's so much better than any of my novels.

"I don't get it." I say, brows furrowed. "Why do you like me? It doesn't make any sense. I was kinda mean to you."

He chews on the side of his lip. "I guess it's time I told you my secret."

"Oookaayy..." Not sure why that's important right now, but if he wants to talk about it, I guess I won't say anything.

He turns to his back, releasing me for one second before grabbing my hand. His free hand pulls out something from his pocket. I can't see what it is in the dim lighting, but I can make out the shape of a heart.

Rolling on his shoulder—our hands still locked—he dangles the object in front of my face. I sit up, taking the plastic purple-and-pink beads from him. Since I let go of his hand, he sits up too, cradling my back, his fingers clutching my un-hurt side.

"Where did you get this?" I say, tears brimming my eyes.

My Disney Princess locket, the one he stole when I was six years old.

"It's been my most prized possession forever, but it was broken. I asked Shaun to get some stuff to help me fix it when I came here. That's why we went to his house the other day."

No way. No, no, no.

Celebrity Superhero

One salty wet drop squeezes from my tear duct. "How, why?"

Caleb leans his head on my shoulder and takes one of my hands. "Because I love you."

The words are so small. I see them almost every day, written on the internet, spoken between fictional characters, doodled on notebooks, but right now, they're huge. So big they fill my heart until I swear it's going to burst. I spin around so we're facing each other.

"Why me?"

Caleb eases the necklace from my grip and ties it around my wrist. It was made for little girls so it doesn't fit around my neck. "I've loved you since we were children. When we moved back to Korea, I was devastated about leaving you. I stole your necklace so I wouldn't forget you. Then I sent you emails. I wrote to you almost every day. You never wrote back so I figured you weren't interested, but you also didn't reject me so I never stop trying."

Could it be true? I search those dark, sparkling eyes, wanting to know if he's being real.

"Your parents always updated my parents about you. I wanted to forget." He shakes his head. "I never could. Even as I came here, I hoped to finally let you go. But you were so amazing. Those stupid glasses, and your silly hair, and that wit of yours. You totally got me. You were even more incredible than I remembered."

I still don't understand. Caleb picked me? Me!

He laughs. "Every time your parents sent us stories or pictures I'd hunger for each one. I'd stay up studying your face, loving your personality more each time. I wanted you to be awful when I came here, wanted to hate you so that I could move on. But you were so spunky I fell in love all over again. How could I not love you?"

My cheeks are streaked with tears, chest heaving. What can I say to that? I love him too. I love him so much it hurts. I'm pretty sure my heart exploded, for real. Never did I think anyone would say that to me. I can't find the words to tell him I love him too, but somehow it must be said.

"I have a secret as well," I say.

Caleb searches my face, lacing our fingers together and squeezing. "What is that?"

This may ruin everything, but I've already come this far. "From the moment you debuted with SUPER, I've been obsessed with you. I've watched all of your videos countless times, learned all your dances, followed the movements of your career. Even with every other handsome K-pop star out there, I only saw you. Caleb—"

I want to say more but Caleb cuts me off with a kiss. His fingers weave into my hair, his other arm curling around my back, pressing me closer. Our lips part, but only just.

"I love you, Caleb," I say against his skin.

His mouth captures mine, and we can't get enough. All this time we've starved for each other. I take his neck in my hands, rubbing the fuzzy hair at the base of his head. Our chins tilt, lips pressing harder. Caleb wiggles until he's free of his sleeping bag, and then he pulls me into his lap.

I let out a little yelp of surprise, but don't stop kissing. His fingers are digging into my spine, pulling me closer until there's no space left. Oh, how I want him. I can't believe he wants me too.

The lights burst on, and Caleb falls backward causing me to land across him sideways. Busted.

"Just what do you two think you're doing?" Dad says.

We both sit up, but Caleb still won't let go of my hand. One squeeze lets me know that come what may, Caleb isn't leaving my side.

Dad's look says I'm going to be grounded for a year. Somehow, it's okay.

Caleb loves me. Even if he has to leave for his career, even if we only see each other through Skype most of the time, even if half the world separates us, everything will be fine. We've loved each other this long and we're not going to stop now. No matter what the future brings, we'll fight through it. Together.

# Happily Ever After

The theater smells of smoke machines. Confetti litters the seats and walkways. I never imagined I'd get to see SUPER live with Erin by side. Much less with Sungwook as my boyfriend. It hasn't been easy being away from him for an entire year, but not a day has passed that we haven't either Skyped or FaceTimed. Now, he's finishing up his first North American tour in Portland and he's planning on spending the rest of the week with me.

"Anna?" the security guard asks, seeing the lanyard around my neck.

Erin pats my shoulder. "I'll meet you out at the car."

Caleb extended his stay in America for another week and he greeted Erin in person, asking her if it was okay that we were dating. She gave us her permission.

I give her a nod, and watch as she heads to the stairs and out of the theater.

"You can head backstage now," the security guard says.

I give him a nod, climbing the steps to the stage and heading behind the curtain.

I'm barely past the rigging when I spot Caleb still wearing the fitted suit for their last number. He hasn't taken off his headset microphone yet, and drops of sweat gather around his brow. He holds what looks like a bouquet, but it's made of leaves. The light from the door behind him frames his excellent figure.

Even though we've been together for a year, even though I've spent every day, sometimes late at night, talking with him, I still haven't wrapped my head around the fact that he's mine. He's too amazing to belong with me. I'm afraid to touch him for fear he'll disappear like vapor. But then, he opens his arms.

I take a deep breath and put my hand to my chest like I'm still unsure that he's choosing me. He nods, gesturing like he can't wait for me to come to him.

My feet can't carry me to him fast enough. He scoops me up and lifts me around, dropping what he's holding to the floor. I brush my fingers along the place where his hair meets his neck, and he holds my gaze.

"I still can't believe you're real," he says to me, but I wanted to say that to him first.

"I still can't believe you like me," I say instead.

He licks his lips, moving his face closer to mine. "Not *like*, love."

I close the space between us, knowing this hunger can never be fulfilled. I can't imagine a day when I won't want him with the same intensity I want him now. Even if that day comes, I can't picture a time when he still won't mean the world to me.

After he left for Korea, I found the password to my childhood email address and read every letter he sent me. His love poured through each page.

"Hang on," he says, breaking our kiss way before I'm ready.

He sets me down and picks up the bouquet. "Remember these?" he asks, showing me the leaves.

170

I take them from him and run my hands over the waxy surface. "Are these from our bush?"

One corner of his mouth turns up, and I smack him with the branches. "Why would you do that?"

He raises his eyebrows, and then pecks me on the cheek. I totally blush, covering the place where his lips touched mine. He remembered the place we hid from the sasaengs that one day and made a bouquet out of it for me.

"Because," he says, "that was the moment when I first realized I would never love anyone else. Anna, you're it for me. The one."

I smack him with the bouquet one more time. He rips it from my hands then picks me up again, and this time I wrap my legs around his hips.

"Now," he says, "where were we?"

"I was telling you how much I cared, with my lips," I tease.

"You're right," he says, "We should get back to that."

And we do. We get back to it for as long as time will allow.

# Celebrity Superhero

If you loved this book, please leave a review!

If you'd like to sign up for my newsletter and get a free book, click here.

# Acknowledgements

It's always hard for me to write this part because so many people go into the making of a single book. As I reflect back on everyone involved in this process, I get a little teared up knowing I wouldn't be here without them.

First, I have to thank Abby Eom. She's the person I wrote this story for. I based this character off her and her love for fiction. I'll have to apologize for changing her name, but she can't be the same person as the bratty friend in Undercover Fan. I love you, Abby!

My next shout-out is to Erica Laurie who's held my hand through this entire self-publishing rollercoaster, and signed up to be my copy-editor. Honestly, amazing people like her are hard to find, and I'm glad she's on my team.

To my beta book peeps who truly are the reason I've published anything. Jenny Morris, Cassie Mae, Teresa Marie, Kelly Lynn, Suzi Retzlaff, Jessica Salyer, Lizzy Charles, Leigh Covington, and Hope Roberson, I know I say this every time, but you all rock!

Emily Bogner, it was wonderful to meet you at Storymakers. I'm so happy you asked to read this for me and so quickly. You are a true hero!

Y'all, Precy Larkins is the best editor on the face of the planet. I recommend her to any authors who are looking to self-publish. She truly is the exact kick-in-the-pants I always need to get my books into good shape. Thank you, my beautiful love!

Who would I be if I didn't thank the very people who make my earth turn? To my husband, my confidant, the love of my existence. I chose you, and I always will.

My kids fill my days with both joy and fury, and I love every second of it. I dedicated this book to them because my nine-year-old was sitting next to me as I wrote the dedication and he asked me to. I would do anything for them. Love you to infinity.

I not only believe in God, but I know of His reality. His Son came to this earth and died for me. He died for you, too, and He lives again. Writing a book might not seem like something an all-powerful omniscient being would care about, but I testify that He guided me through this process and inspired me as I both wrote and edited this work. He cares. Even about the miniscule things.

Most importantly, thank you, dear reader, for reading. I've had the privilege of getting to know a few of you better and you're just as amazing as I envisioned you to be. You picking up this book means the world to me. Thank you, thank you, thank you.

Reviews enable me to write more books. Would you take a minute and review this on Amazon, Bookbub, or Goodreads? It would mean so much. Thank you!

# About the Author

Jennie Bennett is a mother to four beautiful and crazy children, and wife to a handsome and kind husband. She found a passion in Korean pop culture in January of 2013 and she's never looked back since. She currently resides in Houston, Texas with her husband, kids, and a cute puppy named Charlie.

Twitter: @jabennettwrites

Facebook: Jennie Bennett

Instagram: @jenniefire

Come join my newsletter and get free books!
https://www.subscribepage.com/b3f6u5

Celebrity Superhero

Jennie Bennett

Made in the USA
Columbia, SC
28 December 2019